"If my
needs
murmured

Now convinced Ruthie was awake, Robert didn't pull away when she reached for him again. Then he nearly lost it when she said hoarsely, "I want your hands all over me."

"Here?" Robert whispered against her neck, moving his palm until it scraped her pebbled nipple under the lace.

"Yes. Please, yes."

She didn't have to ask him twice. He pushed her camisole up, and he was unable to withhold a smile of male satisfaction as her breasts fell free. She moaned when he slid his hands over them, catching her nipples with his fingers. Then, unable to wait, he lowered his mouth, replacing his fingers with his lips.

She nearly came apart. "I need you," she whispered, reaching down to the waistband of his trousers. Realizing Ruthie wasn't in the mood for slow and easy, Robert followed her lead, undoing his slacks and letting her push them from his hips.

As he stepped back to get the condom from his pocket, Ruthie finally opened her eyes. "Oh, my." She stared at his blatant arousal and a smile curved her lips. "I've never dreamed of quite so...much before."

Dear Reader,

Hot sex with a gorgeous stranger. Not exactly P.C. these days, but it's still such a naughty, delicious fantasy that I just had to explore the concept for Temptation.

Ruthie Sinclair is the girl next door, the girl who is everybody's best friend, who bemoans her hair, her weight and her miserable love life. So when she finds herself in bed with the most amazing man she's ever— make that *never*—known, she's completely out of her element. And Robert Kendall, a man used to corporate piranhas, finds himself way over his head when confronted with a zany, redheaded temptress who makes him hotter than any woman he's ever met.

Their love affair is torrid. Outrageous. Flamboyant. Wow, I had loads of fun writing this one!

I so enjoyed hearing from readers after my first release, Temptation #747, *Night Whispers*. Please drop me a line and let me know what you think of my follow-up book. You can e-mail me through my Web site: www.lesliekelly.com, or write to P.O. Box 410787, Melbourne, FL 32941-0787.

All the best,

Leslie Kelly

SUITE SEDUCTION
Leslie Kelly

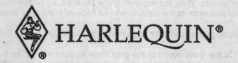

HARLEQUIN®

TORONTO • NEW YORK • LONDON
AMSTERDAM • PARIS • SYDNEY • HAMBURG
STOCKHOLM • ATHENS • TOKYO • MILAN • MADRID
PRAGUE • WARSAW • BUDAPEST • AUCKLAND

To my editor, Brenda Chin. Thanks for letting me have another turn on this crazy, wonderful merry-go-round.

And to Betty. You knew I could, and I really did. How I wish you were here to see it.

ISBN 0-373-25910-7

SUITE SEDUCTION

1

IF Ruthie Sinclair could have wrapped her hands around the throat of the genius who'd composed "The Wedding March," the guy would be six feet under. Every note resounding from the bowels of the organ in the eaves of the church pierced into her skull like the prick of a needle, grating on her nerves until her eyelids twitched. Not an easy feat considering the bride's makeup consultant had coated about a pound of thick, black mascara onto her lashes.

"I'm really starting to hate this song," she muttered through gritted teeth, earning a glance from her cousin Denise, the other bridesmaid. The blonde shook her head, a disapproving frown on her brow, and gestured toward the bride, who stood a few feet away in the vestibule. Luckily, she hadn't heard.

Ruthie knew she should be happy. Her cousin and best friend, Celeste, was marrying the man of her dreams. For a woman who considered herself a cockeyed optimist, the fairy-tale happy ending should have had Ruthie cheering and doing cartwheels. And she would...when she stopped feeling so darned depressed.

"Smile! Maybe you'll catch the bouquet," Denise whispered. The words might have been meant to cheer her up, but the tone was pure Denise—pure sugar-coated spite. "Like when you caught *mine* two months ago."

Ruthie's teeth hurt as she tried to pull her face into a smile. "I sure was excited about that, you can bet." Especially when she got to dance with the twelve-year-old junior usher who caught the garter—his nosy little eyeballs had come right to the center of her cleavage!

A wicked light shone in Denise's eyes, and, not for the first time, Ruthie wondered if they were truly related. Maybe Denise was adopted. Or maybe Ruthie was. That would explain the more eccentric Sinclairs who sometimes led her to believe she'd fallen into an episode of a TV sitcom.

When she considered some of her other family members, one catty, obnoxious blonde wasn't too surprising. The only surprising part was that Denise was Celeste's older sister. Ruthie's younger cousin, the bride, was real sugar to Denise's saccharine, real class to her sister's pretension.

Ruthie had nailed Denise's real character years ago, when her cousin had *accidentally* dropped a big wad of bubble gum in Ruthie's hair. In the middle of the night. When she was supposed to be sleeping in another cabin at their summer camp. Ruthie had spent that year looking like the freckle-faced kid on the Cracker Jack box, short red hair and all. Then there was the time Denise had locked Ruthie in a freight elevator. And the time Denise had put toothpaste in Ruthie's bottle of peppermint foot lotion.

And today. Ruthie glanced down and grimaced as she once again beheld how hideous she looked. Yes, she would be willing to bet Denise had a hand in today's debacle: a bridal-shop error that had landed her in what had to be the butt-ugliest bridesmaid dress in the annals of wedding history.

"Maybe if you catch it twice in a row, Bobby will get the hint," Denise said, a note of amused malice in her voice.

Celeste walked up and overheard her sister's comment. "As if Bobby needs any hints about how wonderful Ruthie is! Denise, you'd better check your makeup, your green is showing through."

Denise smirked, then walked away. Ruthie's frown deepened. "I've come to the conclusion that Bobby doesn't take hints very well. I've all but popped out of a cake in a G-string and pasties and he still hasn't...." Ruthie caught a glimpse of the minister in the front of the church and felt her face go red. "I'm sorry, I can't believe I said that in here!"

Celeste squeezed her hand in commiseration. "Maybe hinting's not the right approach. I'd say it's time to be direct. Maybe he hasn't been reading your signals."

Ruthie figured any man would have to be completely clueless not to have realized she was interested in a more serious relationship after four months of dating. Conservative, quiet, and subdued he may be, but he *was* an adult male.

Still, at this point, seeing not only Denise and Celeste marry within months of each other, but also the remarriage of her own *mother*, she was willing to try just about anything!

Forcing a smile to her lips, she winked at Celeste, then prepared to begin the procession. As she passed, Denise simpered at her. "Don't trip in that *lovely* gown, now, Ruthie."

Ruthie grimaced. Lovely? Yeah, right. *Denise* looked

lovely. She, at least, was wearing the right dress. Its dusty rose color set off her pale skin and ash-blond curls to perfection. Ruthie, on the other hand, looked utterly ridiculous. Like a breakfast sausage link found in the bottom of a dirty old refrigerator. Moldy, green and puffy.

Ignoring her cousin, as she had most of her life, Ruthie took a deep breath and walked beneath the archway to the aisle. "Just get through the wedding, then you can go back to the hotel and drink enough champagne to work up the nerve to make a serious pass at Bobby," she told herself.

Maybe Celeste was right. Perhaps the time had come to be direct with Bobby. And tonight would be the perfect time, at the romantic reception held in the wonderful old hotel that was a huge part of Ruthie's life. Her family's pride and joy, the Kerrigan Towers was the perfect spot to seduce a man.

Celeste's father, Ruthie's uncle, was the manager of the Kerrigan, and had given every member of the bridal party a room for the night. So a seduction could be carried out easily.

It had come as no surprise when Celeste decided to have her reception at the hotel. The Kerrigan had been owned by the Sinclair family for decades. And, like Ruthie, Celeste worked in the hotel, handling the business side of things in the cashier's office, while Ruthie indulged all her creative urges as the head chef in the hotel kitchens. Celeste had even planned her wedding for a Sunday to be sure everyone would be able to get the evening off, since Saturdays were just too busy.

Casting one more glance over her shoulder, Ruthie saw the joy in Celeste's face. She wanted that feeling, the feeling of being loved...being *in* love! She wanted it very badly.

So, seduction at the Kerrigan it would be. She was ready. She could do it. She was a mature, confident woman, a talented chef, a respected hotel board member. None of which changed the fact that she was probably going to make a major fool of herself. *But it's worth a shot!*

Giving her flirty lace parasol a spin over her shoulder, she proceeded to march. Right foot. Pause. Left foot. Pause. Concentrate on Celeste's happiness. Pause. Forget Denise. Pause. Stop imagining what a fool she was going to appear if Bobby turned her down. Pause. Forget her cousins were happily married and she couldn't even get her boyfriend to cop a feel. Pause. Forget her miserable romantic track record. Pause.

Not to mention her butt-ugly dress.

ROBERT KENDALL felt a trickle of sweat slide from his hairline, through the slight indentation at his temple, and on down his cheek. The din of conversation and tinkling glasses in the crowded hotel bar receded as he focused on his companion, Monica Winchester. And what she'd just handed him. "Your room key?"

Of course it was her room key. He stared dumbly at the small object as if it was a venomous insect about to inject poison into the vulnerable flesh of his right palm.

"I was hoping for a more...enthusiastic response."

Swallowing hard, Robert finally looked at the other item, the small square on which the key rested. The foil package was unmistakable. Not his brand. Probably not his size. But absolutely recognizable.

"You haven't said anything." Monica's voice gained an edge. "Surely you aren't surprised by this."

He looked at the woman seated across from him at the lounge table. Not surprised? How could he *not* be surprised that his boss's daughter had handed him her room key—and a *condom*—and practically ordered him to show up in her room that night?

"Come on, Robert, we're two consenting adults. We're in a strange city, stuck in this drafty old hotel for who knows how long. Why don't we enjoy ourselves while we can?"

Robert stifled the first answer that popped into his head: *Gee, maybe because the last Winchester Hotels employee you enjoyed yourself with ended up on the unemployment line.*

Instead, he stalled, picking up his vodka tonic and bringing the glass to his lips. He sipped, his mind working overtime to think of a graceful way out of this predicament.

"Monica, obviously I'm flattered," he said, knowing a lot of men in his situation would jump at what she offered. No question, the woman had an earthy, direct sexiness that would appeal to a lot of men—until they got to know her. "But I don't think it's a good idea to mix pleasure with business."

Monica Winchester, obviously not used to being turned down, waved her hand in disregard. "I'm barely involved in the business. I talked my way into this trip for one reason only."

Robert's eyes narrowed as she confirmed his suspicion about her motives for insisting she come to Philadelphia with him to check out the Kerrigan Towers. "I wondered about that."

She smiled broadly. In the dim light of the smoky room her white teeth were predatory. "You're my father's golden boy, Robert. The son he's never had. He relies on you and would like nothing better than for you to become a part of his family. Why do you think he's been trying so hard to set us up?"

"Pairing us at dinner parties and inviting me for holidays isn't quite the same as handing me a condom and a room key," Robert said as he gestured to the waiter for another drink.

She chuckled. "It's not like it's an engagement ring. Why can't we test the waters, see if we're compatible?"

"Couples generally see if they're compatible by going out on a few dates, catching a movie, maybe some dinner."

"I'm not going to waste time having dinner with a man who doesn't cut it for me in bed."

Before the waiter could place the fresh drink on the table, Robert grabbed the glass and downed a third of its contents.

"I've surprised you." Her amused tone annoyed him no small amount. "Listen, I have a few calls to make, then I plan to take a hot bubble bath. You stay here, have a drink or two, and come up when you're ready. My room number's on the key tag."

"Monica..." he said as she stood and reached for her bag.

"Don't say anything now you might regret later, Robert." He wondered if he heard a threat in her voice. *Sleep with me or I'll get my daddy to fire you?* It seemed ridiculous, of course. Ridiculous, but not impossible.

"I'll see you later." Not content to just walk away, she bent over and lightly kissed him. *"Don't* disappoint me."

A half hour and an additional drink later, Robert glanced at his watch, debating his course of action. Going to her room was out of the question. He could not

have a one-night stand with James Winchester's
daughter. The man had earned Robert's respect in the
eight years they'd worked together. He'd trusted Robert from the first, when he'd been another fresh-from-
Grad-school know-it-all who wanted to change the
world. Or own it.

Maybe he hadn't changed the world, but he *had*
helped mold Winchester Hotels into the fastest-rising
chain in the country. Not bad for a country boy from
North Carolina, who'd never even stayed in a classy
hotel until he'd graduated from college.

His parents hadn't understood his need to get away,
to go live in New York City, of all places, leaving behind his five siblings, assorted aunts, uncles and cousins, and the family auto repair business. But Robert
had been born with wandering feet, with dreams of
building things, maybe even with a bit of a shark's
killer instinct.

Those qualities had served him well in his years
working for Winchester Hotels. And James Winchester
was not cheap about showing his appreciation. Plus,
Robert genuinely liked the man. He couldn't repay him
by sleeping with his "little angel."

Standing the little angel up, however, seemed infi-
nitely more dangerous. Especially now, during a deli-
cate scouting expedition of this grand old Philadelphia
hotel. The Kerrigan Towers would transition nicely
into a Winchester Hotel. But not if Monica threw a fit
and sabotaged their critical meeting with the current
owners the next morning. If she walked in playing corporate prima donna, the board, most of them members
of the Sinclair family, would close ranks and fight the
inevitable.

One thing he could not do was sit in the bar any

longer. Dropping a tip on the table, he left the lounge and entered the deserted corridor. Working in the business had him paying attention to all the details other guests would never notice. The pale blue carpet in the hall was worn—clean, but threadbare after years of being walked upon by the hotel's elite clientele. The plastered ceiling was yellowed, showing signs of spidery cracks that had been hastily repaired. He took mental note that the walls needed paint, and the rickety elevator groaned like an overworked old woman. Heck, even rooms in need of electronic keys to replace the archaic metal ones, like the one burning a hole in the right pocket of his sports coat!

The Kerrigan Towers was ripe for the plucking. And Robert had come to Philadelphia to pluck.

Noticing the lobby was deserted, he decided to do some snooping. Robert knew exactly where he needed to go. One of the most important spots to investigate in any hotel was the kitchen. He'd seen dozens of seemingly elegant establishments with ovens dirtier than any 24-hour roadside diner.

Since his reason for visiting the Kerrigan was hush-hush, at least until tomorrow's board meeting, he certainly couldn't ask for a tour. Now, just after midnight, seemed a good time to investigate. No one would be around, no one would be the wiser.

Robert slipped stealthily into the closed restaurant. Dodging between the backs of cushioned chairs, he took note of his surroundings. So far so good. The floor looked pristine. The air smelled sweet of fresh-cut flowers and well-prepared food. A hint of pine cleanser also indicated cleanliness, without being cloying or antiseptic.

Pushing quietly through the swinging doors, he

looked around, assessing how well he could see in the darkened kitchen. But the room wasn't completely dark. In the far corner, he saw a single light burning, and wondered if it was left on as a security measure. Walking gingerly on the tile floor to avoid making any noise, he made his way toward the light.

A hiccuping sob told him he was not alone.

"Please let me forget what an absolute fool I made of myself tonight!"

He froze.

"Please let me close my eyes and pretend I'm not a whiny, pathetic woman in an ugly green dress."

Hidden in the shadows of a huge wall oven, Robert studied the woman sitting at a worktable beneath the single light.

Her dress really was damn ugly.

She, however, was quite lovely. She sat on a stool in front of a large, butcher-block table, where the chef probably worked when the restaurant was open. Her bare feet rested on the top rung of the stool, and her dress was haphazardly gathered in a mound of green fluff on her lap. Her legs were enough to stop his breath. Sweet, so sweet, encased in what appeared to be white thigh-high stockings that ended with a flirtatious bit of lace just below the edge of her hefted-up gown.

"Maybe one more bite," the woman muttered. Robert bit the inside of his cheek to stop a laugh as he saw her plunge a fork into about half of what had once been a very large chocolate cake. She brought a portion to her mouth, letting out a pleased sigh as she bit off little pieces of it. Her tongue flicked out to lick the icing from the metal tines of the fork, and Robert had to swallow hard to contain the moan of appreciation he felt sure was going to spill across his lips.

She closed her eyes, dropping her head back, and he continued studying her, noting the long, smooth line of her throat, the generous curve of her hip, and the indentation of her waist in the tight dress. Not to mention the gorgeous, full breasts so magnificently displayed in the low-cut gown.

The overhead bulb caught the highlights in the mass of red curls surrounding her face. Judging by the beaded headpiece lying on the table, and the scattering of bobby pins beside it, she'd just taken her hair down and allowed most of it to fall freely in a soft curtain about her shoulders.

Lovely shoulders. She was soft-looking, with the pale skin of a redhead and the curves of a real man's fantasy. Not thin and angular, no, she was rounded and curvaceous like an old-time movie starlet. Maybe not the fashion today, but so physically appealing to Robert he suddenly found it difficult to draw breath.

He heard her grunt, and watched as she opened her eyes and began struggling with her dress. As she pushed down on the mound of fabric on her lap, the sides poufed out, nearly forming an O-shape. Robert stifled a chuckle as he realized what she was wearing. It appeared, from where he stood, to be one of those god-awful southern belle style bridesmaid gowns.

"I swear as soon as I get home you're going to get a taste of my shears. Though I don't dislike my neighbors enough to make curtains out of you," the woman said as she finally subdued the dress hoop. "No wonder the south lost—there wasn't any room for men with every woman taking up ten feet of floor space!"

This time, Robert wasn't able to contain the chuckle.

RUTHIE HELD the crushed dress tightly against her thighs and was reaching for the long neck of an expensive bottle of champagne when she heard a very masculine laugh. "Who's there?" she asked, immediately hopping up from the stool and bumping her hip into the edge of her worktable. "Ouch."

"Are you all right?"

She peered into the dark recesses of the kitchen, finally seeing one shadow separate itself from beyond the huge, stainless steel refrigerator. A figure approached her in the darkness. It had to be a man, she assumed, because of the height. He moved slowly, silently, almost gliding across the floor like something supernatural. She'd never met such a tall man who moved with such grace. Ruthie tensed as visions of a vampire movie she'd recently watched on cable flooded her muddled brain.

"Who are you?" she asked sharply as her fingers skittered across the table toward the knife block. She'd just about decided on the meat cleaver when she heard his warm laugh again.

"I'm sorry, I really didn't mean to intrude." The man stepped closer until he walked into the small pool of light cast by the overhead fixture. Then, when he was fully illuminated, Ruthie could only manage a sigh.

He was like something out of a *GQ*-inspired fantasy. Tall. So tall she'd have to tilt her head all the way back to look up at him. His hair was thick, wavy, the rich brown of her very best *au jus*. The face was classically handsome, smooth-shaven, cleanly shaped with high, strong cheekbones that drew attention to the heavily lashed, dark brown eyes. His face was creased by a broad smile outlined by a pair of lips so sensual they were made to be kissed. Her own lips parted, puckered slightly, of their own free will, as she continued to examine him.

He wore a navy sports coat, tailored to highlight the shoulders that seemed too wide to fit through any standard doorway. His white dress shirt, open at the throat, revealed tanned skin and a hint of chest hair. Ruthie had always found that particular spot fascinating on a man, particularly one as well built as this one. Not that she had inspected any up close anytime recently. Like within the past three years.

Light gray slacks, tailored to fit him perfectly, skimmed his lean hips. They were expensive, obviously, but also tight enough to leave her speculating that he wore boxers, not briefs.

"I'm dreaming," she finally managed to say, shaking her head mournfully. "I've fallen asleep, my face is right now resting cheekbone high in a six-inch tall cake, and in the morning someone's going to come in and find I've asphyxiated myself on Ghirardelli."

He grinned. "I'm very real, I'm afraid. We seem to have had the same idea. Sneaking into the kitchen for a late-night snack?"

Ruthie shook her head, trying to sort through the champagne-inspired cobwebs clouding her thoughts. "I needed some serious chocolate," she finally said.

He held her eye and slowly nodded. "I think I do, too."

Ruthie grabbed a fork from a stack of washed dishes on a nearby counter and tossed it to him. "Help yourself."

He caught it easily, sat on another stool next to the one she'd vacated, and dug right in.

Ruthie watched a smile of satisfaction cross his face as he tasted. Okay, he was real. He wasn't a vampire.

Vampires didn't eat food, except, maybe, raw steak. Certainly not sweets. And this guy obviously appreciated the cake. Another point in his favor, considering she'd made it!

"Have some champagne," she said as she sat next to him on the other stool. "There's more where that came from."

He glanced at the half-empty bottle, and the full one standing next to it, raising an inquisitive eyebrow.

"Spoils from the wedding."

He dropped his stare to her dress. "I gathered as much."

She grimaced as she looked down at the bunched-up material on her lap. "Had to be, huh? I guess I can't pass for a seventeen-year-old, so you'd never have figured I was a dumped prom date."

"Dumped? Never."

"Maybe not a prom date. But dumped." Ruthie heard a tiny whine in her voice and hated it.

"Only if the guy's a complete and utter moron."

She tried to take comfort in the conviction in his voice, but, remembering her evening, could do nothing but frown. "It's not him. It's me. I'm just not desirable."

A look that could only be described as incredulous crossed the man's features. "How much champagne have you had?"

"Not enough to make me forget this stupid dress and the look on his face when I..."

"Yes?"

"Not enough to make me forget this stupid dress," she repeated, forcing herself not to mention how Bobby had reacted when she'd asked him to spend the night with her in her suite.

Shocked wasn't quite the word she'd use to describe his expression. More like horrified.

"I take it the bride didn't want any competition," the man said as he hefted the champagne and took a healthy swig straight from the bottle. Ruthie grinned, seeing a few drops trickling down his chin. Her grin faded as he lowered the bottle and caught the droplets with his tongue. *Oh my, how very agile!*

"I'm sorry?"

He waved a hand toward her dress. "You know. She didn't want her bridesmaids to look *too* good."

"Hence this awful dress that's the same color as the stuff in my one-month-old godson's diapers?"

The gorgeous stranger coughed as he choked on the piece of cake he'd just put in his mouth. Ever helpful, Ruthie leaned forward and gave him a good solid whack on the back. "Okay?"

"Yeah," he muttered. "Sorry...got a strange visual there."

"Can't be any worse than what I've been picturing ever since I showed up at the dress shop two weeks ago and found *this*, instead of the emerald-green gown I was supposed to be wearing! I think they call it 'olive' but it's obviously 'strained peas.' Wrong color. Wrong size. Wrong style, even though I did agree to wear the stupid hoops to please Celeste's future mother-in-law. She's a little old-fashioned."

"The bride?"

Ruthie shook her head. "Celeste? No, she's wonderful. And more into *Modern Bride* than *Southern Weddings!*"

"She doesn't seem the type to inflict hoop skirts and bows on her friends."

"She's not. But she married a great man with a

sweet, craftsy mother, whom she really wanted to please. So Denise and I were stuck playing Suellen and Coreen to Celeste's Scarlett."

"Denise?"

"Another cousin, her older sister," Ruthie explained. A loud sigh escaped her lips. "She got married, too."

"Tonight?"

"No, two months ago. To a very successful, rich guy, who happens to be much too nice for her, but who is also about three inches shorter than Denise!" She heard a note of satisfaction in her own voice. "Sorry, I'm not usually spiteful."

"Denise the bad seed in your clan?"

Ruthie thought about it. "I guess not. A little sneaky, sometimes mean-spirited. Not truly bad. Just very competitive, since we're only a few months apart in age. She does tend to flash her two-carat diamond at me an awful lot."

"And you're the only single one left?"

Ruthie plunged her fork in and hoisted another hunk of cake into her mouth. "Even my sixty-year-old *mother* got married last year. She's now touring the western part of the country in a camper with her new husband, Sid, and his four Scottie dogs," she muttered after she swallowed. "And here I sit. Single. Undesirable. Alone."

The man grabbed her hand as she reached for the bottle. He held it tightly, forcing her to look at him. "If some guy turned you down, it was his own stupidity. You are one amazingly attractive woman, in spite of your..."

"Butt-ugly dress?" she volunteered softly, somewhat awed by the intensity of his stare as he studied her face, her mussed hair, her chocolate-smudged lips.

He laughed, bringing her hand to his mouth to press a kiss on the tips of her fingers. They literally tingled at the warm contact. "Butt-ugly dress or not, the guy's an idiot. He obviously didn't know what he was turning down."

She tugged her hand away. "Oh, yes, he knew," she said sourly. "He knew very well. I handed him my room key and came right out and asked him to spend the night with me."

The man coughed again, making a funny choking sound. Again, Ruthie leaned forward and whacked his back. "Okay?"

"Yeah," he muttered. "Fine. Uh, you handed him your key?"

She nodded. "We've been dating for four months, for heaven's sake. It's not like I'm some stranger trying to pick him up in a hotel bar! But he looked at me like he was appalled." She shook her head, regret drawing her brows down over her eyes. "I knew he was conservative. It's been sheer misery trying to act like I am, too."

"Why would you have to act like anything but who you are?"

"Who I am doesn't seem to work, judging by the completely nonexistent sex life I've had for the past three years." Ruthie clapped a hand over her mouth, unable to believe she'd said something so personal to a complete stranger.

He didn't seem the least bit fazed by her confession. "So you took action?"

"I thought I'd go for a different image," she admitted, finally realizing what an idiot she'd been to try to fit herself into the mold Bobby seemed to want filled. She ruthlessly reached up and pulled at another bobby pin in her hair, tugging a few red strands out with it. "I even tried to tame this mess. But, I'll tell you, if I never have to wear a bun or French twist again, it'll be too soon!"

He reached out a hand and fingered a curl hanging next to her ear, stroking it lightly. Knowing her hair was wildly tangled, she self-consciously moved back until the strands slipped free from his fingers.

"It'd be a crime to hide this," he murmured. "Other than the curls, what else would you want to change?"

Ruthie looked down at herself and frowned. "Maybe the ten extra pounds sitting on my hips and chest that couldn't be blasted off with dynamite?" she muttered.

This time, he didn't chuckle. He laughed, loud and long. "You have got to be kidding. Honey, women pay plastic surgeons buckets of money to get what you've got!"

"I'm not an exotic dancer," she said sourly.

"You could be," he shot back.

Ruthie's breath froze in her throat at the intensity in his stare. He ran his gaze over her entire body, messy hair down to her feet. She realized that within a five-minute acquaintance this man was looking at her in a way Bobby never had the entire time they were dating.

Like he wanted to devour her.

Swallowing hard, Ruthie took another bite of cake. She was sitting alone in a darkened kitchen with a complete stranger—a gorgeous stranger, granted—but she didn't know anything about him. This interlude went against every rule her mother had ever taught her. She wondered why she didn't care.

"I don't know why I'm telling you this," she said with a self-conscious smile.

"Maybe telling me your troubles is easier than admitting them to someone who knows you well? Keep talking, I have nowhere else I'd rather be, and I'm a good listener."

Ruthie was unable to hide the tears springing up in the corners of her eyes. Here she was in the company of this breathtakingly handsome man, and he was watching her with those soulful brown eyes, gentle, interested, sexy as hell. And she was blubbering over another guy, one she couldn't even say she was really attracted to in the first place!

She knew better than anyone the main reason she'd attempted to move her relationship with Bobby to another level: she wanted commitment, wanted happily ever after like Celeste and Denise. Even if it was with a man who was nice instead of thrilling, sweet instead of desirable, friendly instead of hot enough to melt the clothes right off her body! Sleeping with Bobby had seemed important because it was a natural progression in a long-term relationship. There'd been no fire. No passionate sparks. Ruthie had thought being with him would be comfortable, nice, sedate. Like Bobby himself.

Seduction had seemed like a good idea. He, judging by the shocked expression on his face when she'd handed him her key, didn't agree.

Ruthie started sniffling again, not only because of her teary eyes but also because of a bad case of springtime allergies that had been plaguing her for days. She reached up and wiped her nose with the back of her hand, not even caring that another one of her mother's rules went flying out the window. Her fingers came away with a smudge of chocolate, and she realized she must have had a mustache over her lips. "Oh, great, I look like Charlie Chaplin, don't I?" This time she couldn't stop the fat tears that rolled out of her eyes, down her cheeks and landed with a plop on the butcher-block table.

The beautiful man moved his hand to her face, cupped her chin with infinite gentleness and turned her head. Forcing her to look at him, he leaned closer, so close she could smell the chocolate and champagne on his breath, and wondered if her scent was half as intoxicating as his.

"You look lovely to me. And I don't even know your name."

For some reason, his words made the tears come faster, and suddenly the day's events, her loneliness and the blow to her self-confidence crashed in on her with the weight of a ton of cement blocks. "It's Ruthie. My name's Ruthie," she said between sniffs.

He smiled gently and reached toward his pocket. "Here, wipe your tears, Ruth. A woman with eyes as bright and green as yours has no business crying."

Ruthie watched him reach into the pocket of his sports coat and begin to pull out a handkerchief. It occurred to her to be slightly touched by the old-fashioned gesture, since most men she knew didn't carry handkerchiefs anymore.

Before she could say a word, however, he tugged the white cotton fabric free, and with it came a few other objects from his pocket. She heard a clink, looked down, and saw the two items that had landed on the floor between the two stools. They were unmistakable. A key and... "Oh, God," she wailed, "Is everyone in this hotel having sex tonight except me?"

2

IF SHE HADN'T looked so adorably indignant, Robert might have laughed again. He was unable to hide a grin, though, as she threw her crossed arms down on the table in front of her and plopped her head onto them.

Ruthie. Sweet, funny, voluptuous Ruthie. How could he ever have imagined he'd stumble onto such a vibrant woman in the darkened kitchen of a hotel? Or that she'd appeal to him so instantly, so sharply, like no other woman had in years?

For whatever reason, Robert suddenly felt like a kid on Christmas morning, who'd found his favorite gift was one he hadn't even included on his ten page wish list!

Things were definitely looking up. Maybe he would even have reason to look back on Monica's ridiculous offer and be thankful. It had driven him here, to this room, at just the right moment to meet someone who had knocked his socks off in less than fifteen minutes.

Someone who, he realized, was still sniffling as she kept her face buried in her crossed arms.

"No, I'm *definitely* not having sex tonight," he said, confirming that fact not only to her but to himself. "And I haven't had it in a pretty long time, either. So you're not alone. Now, will you please stop crying?"

Her head lifted and she stared at him. Hard. "Why not?"

"Why not what?"

"Why aren't you having sex? You're gorgeous. You're nice. You smell good and you don't have bad breath. Why isn't there some woman waiting for you upstairs?" A sudden look of understanding crossed her face. "Oh, great, you're gay, aren't you? That's it. You're gay. Somebody, just shoot me now."

He bordered on taking offense, but since she was so obviously miserable, not to mention tipsy, he forgave her for momentarily doubting his preferences. "Not gay."

"Married?"

"Nope."

"Sissy mama's boy?"

He cringed. "My mama's a mechanic."

"Why celibate, then?"

That seemed a very good question right now. Particularly since all he'd been able to think about since he'd first seen her licking chocolate off her fork was how much he wanted her to be tasting *him.*

"It's been a long time since I met anyone I was seriously interested in." Not three years, of course. He shuddered at the thought that she'd been unattached for so long. Were men in Philly totally blind? "Why you? Other than the obvious things like your gorgeous red hair has too much curl, and you've got a figure most men with stick-thin girlfriends fantasize about?"

His flattery didn't influence her. She obviously didn't believe it. "I've been busy. Working, helping the family with the business."

"You work with your family?"

She nodded. "It takes a lot of time and energy. Not

that I'm complaining—I love my family a lot. And I do have friends I spend time with."

"But no boyfriends other than the loser who passed up the chance to spend a night with you?"

She sighed. "It's hard to meet eligible men when you work ten hours a day, six days a week."

"I know how that goes. My job requires a lot of travel, not much time for home and family. Not that I mind. That's exactly what I wanted growing up. I couldn't wait to leave home, get away from the craziness of five younger brothers, have my own quiet place, then go out and conquer the world."

"And have you?"

He grinned. "I'm working on it."

They fell silent. It wasn't a heavy, uncomfortable silence between two strangers who'd had a very intimate conversation. Instead, Robert just enjoyed breathing the same air, catching the light scent of her perfume, watching the way the glints of gold in her hair caught the light. *Hearing her sniffle.* "You cryin' again?"

She shook her head. "Allergies."

"Good. I can't stand it when women cry."

Ruthie sighed, her shoulders drooping. "I love to cry. I rate movies by the tissue factor."

"How depressing."

"No," she insisted, "it's not. I don't mean I like to see horror or twisted stuff that brings you down, but there's something so moving about a real love story, doomed and destined to end in tragedy."

"Yeah, they move me, all right," he muttered, "right out of the theater. I like war movies."

"Yuck. Blood and gore. Sat through half of one last year on a blind date and threw up my popcorn and

Sno-Caps right onto his shoes." She sounded very philosophical about the experience.

"Did he ever call again?"

She rolled her eyes and let out an unladylike snort.

"Well," he said, giving his head a rueful shake, "I've had my fair share of bad dates, too."

"But I bet you never got sick on your date's shiny new penny loafers."

"True," he conceded. "But if he was enough of a geek to be wearing penny loafers, he deserved it."

She raised a sardonic brow. "Are you criticizing my taste in men? Implying I date geeks?"

He shook his head and held his hands up, palms out. "No, no, you said he was a blind date, remember? Obviously the friend who set you up doesn't know you very well!"

She smirked. "My mother set us up."

He paused, looking at her out of the corner of his eye, silently daring her to go on.

"Okay, okay, so she *doesn't* know me very well!"

His expression was triumphant. "Nobody's mother knows them very well. That's why mothers love their children when any sane person would have kicked them to the curb years before."

Ruthie nodded in agreement with his reasoning, then said, "Is yours really a mechanic?"

He nodded ruefully. "She and my father are in the auto repair business back home in North Carolina."

"Southern boy," she said as she stuck her fork in the last third of the cake and helped herself to another bite. "I guess that explains the good manners, the handkerchief and all. But no accent?"

"New York eventually wore it away."

Robert reached out to help himself to more cake, and

accidentally tangled his fork with the tines of hers. "Sorry."

"If we were down to the last bite, you'd have to fork-duel me for it. But I think there's enough left for both of us," she said with a huge grin as she disentangled their utensils.

When she truly smiled, she did so with her whole face, not just those beautiful lips. Robert watched her, awed by the transformation genuine amusement brought to her already pretty features. Her eyes sparkled. A pair of adorable dimples turned up in her cheeks. He had forgotten how much of a sucker he'd always been for dimples—had been since his first crush on the freckled, dimpled, toothless Doreen Watson in second grade. Now he was reminded with such sudden, raw joy that he simply didn't know what to say. He merely smiled back, memorizing her features, as though afraid this entire interlude might be a figment of his imagination brought on by one too many vodka tonics and might disappear at any moment.

From outside, Robert heard a few horns beeping. The flash of a blue strobe from a police car passing by the window spotlighted the far wall of the room. Distracted, he looked around. The kitchen was immaculate, reminding him of his original purpose. He'd completely forgotten why he'd come snooping while he'd talked with Ruthie. Amazing. A woman who could actually make him forget about his job, albeit only for twenty minutes or so.

Ruthie finally broke the comfortable silence that had once again fallen between them. "So, I suppose you like sports." Her voice held a note of resignation.

He nodded. "You?"

She shook her head mournfully. "Nope."

"What about music?" he asked, immediately recognizing her bid to see just what they might have in common, other than the *cajones* to sneak into a private hotel kitchen and raid the dessert cabinet.

Her eyes brightened. "I love country-western!"

He cringed. "My father nearly disowned me when I was nine and told him I hated country and liked New-Orleans-style jazz."

A gentle smile and a look of tenderness crossed her face. "My father and I used to sing along to Broadway albums when I was growing up. He had a wonderful voice."

"Had?"

She nodded. "He died when I was in high school." Her voice broke, and she gave her head a quick shake, then reached for the bottle of champagne.

"So," Robert said, trying to move past the awkward moment, "what else? How about books?"

He could have predicted her answer before she said it. "Romances. You?"

"Techno-thrillers."

"I get tired thinking about picking up one of those two-ton hardbacks," she said with a frown. "Do you think those guys get paid by the word?"

Since he'd sometimes wondered the same thing, he nodded. "Seems possible." Instead of being depressed at their conflicting personalities and tastes, Robert found himself thoroughly enjoying their banter.

"Kids!" she exclaimed and he almost heard the "aha" she didn't utter. "Growing up with all those younger brothers, you must *love* children!"

He gave a vehement shake of his head. "Growing up with all those brothers made me *never* want to have children."

Her shoulders sagged. "Really? Maybe you just think you don't want any."

He shuddered. "Ruthie, I practically raised my younger brothers while our parents were getting their business off the ground. Snotty noses, diapers, chicken pox, bad dreams, never-ending fistfights. Believe me, I did all the child-rearing I *ever* want to do before my eighteenth birthday."

She looked at him, studying his face as if testing his sincerity, then a disappointed frown marred her brow. She studied her own hands, suddenly quiet and pensive. "I can't remember a time when I didn't dream about growing up and having lots of children."

Lots? He couldn't even fathom the possibility of *one.* It did seem critically important to her, though. What she wanted for her own future really wasn't any of his business, he supposed. She was an absolute stranger to him; he might never see her again after this one unusual night. But he couldn't stop a feeling of regret over their completely discordant dreams for their futures.

"I hope your dream comes true one day, Ruthie." He hoisted the bottle and held it up for a toast. "To your future babies. May they all be female so you don't have the nightmare of raising *lots* of little boys like I did."

She nodded, grabbed the bottle, and took a liberal sip.

"So, where were we?" he mused. "Ah, yes, what could we possibly we have in common that we can talk about now?"

She squared her shoulders. "What about the weather?"

"I think we've moved a little beyond talking about the weather, Ruthie. After all, I already know the details of your sex life, and you saw a condom fall out of my pocket."

"The details of my *nonexistent* sex life," she retorted, "and thank you *so* much for reminding me!" She rolled her eyes. "For your information, I was talking about the seasons. Are you a summer man or a winter one?"

"Summer. Definitely. Sandy beaches, bright blue sky, waterskiing, deep-sea fishing. Give me ninety and sunny any day." He had a sudden purely delightful mental image of lying on a beach, sipping a fruity rum concoction, watching Ruthie walk toward him from the water, wearing a tiny bikini that barely covered the full, lush curves of her breasts.

He glanced at her, to see if she'd caught the brainless, besotted expression he felt sure must be on his face.

She looked like she wanted to slug him. "Winter," she practically snarled. "Nothing compares to snuggling up in your very softest angora sweater, sipping hot chocolate with marshmallows in front of a roaring fireplace at a beautiful mountaintop ski resort."

Sweater? No, no. That definitely wasn't part of the fantasy. "Better than lying on a beach, listening to the gentle surf, feeling someone rub oil into the hot skin of your back?" he asked, his voice growing husky as he fantasized aloud.

She sighed. "Only if there's a gorgeous young waiter dressed in a loincloth bringing me free piña coladas— and Solarcaine by the case since I would turn red as a lobster in forty-five seconds flat."

"Ever heard of beach umbrellas?"

"Ever heard of sun poisoning?" she shot back. "I'm a dermatologist's poster child."

"No risk of sunburn when lying on a hammock beneath a palm tree in the early evening."

She wasn't teased out of her mood. "Just mosquitoes."

Robert shook his head ruefully, admiring her stubbornness, her honesty, even if it was a bit inspired by champagne. "I give up. You're right. We have nothing in common."

Instead of looking pleased that he'd agreed with her, Ruthie frowned deeply. He heard her sigh and watched her shoulders slump again. "I guess not."

They both extended their forks toward the cake at the same instant. "There's always chocolate," he said with a smile.

"Oh, yes," she agreed. "We'll always have chocolate."

Between the two of them, they killed off the first bottle of champagne and did some damage to the second in the next hour. Robert didn't remember when he'd laughed so hard, all the while shifting in his seat as he reacted physically to the gorgeous redhead fate had thrust right under his nose.

He'd never dated a redhead. He'd never dated a curvy bundle of dimpled femininity. His women, in the past, had tended to be more the corporate shark type. Not by preference, he suddenly realized, but merely by circumstance.

His brothers had been telling him for years to get the hell out of New York before he found himself married to one of the piranhas he'd been dating. Robert didn't worry. He had no intention of marrying anyone. His job was too important to him—and too demanding—to try to find time to share his life with a family. Dating piranhas helped make sure he was never tempted.

He'd never taken a woman home, of course, knowing the full Kendall clan was enough to frighten off
anyone. More than that, he'd never met a woman he'd
wanted to bring to North Carolina. But some members
of his family had met one or two girlfriends when
they'd come to visit him.

"Find a nice southern girl," his mother had said after
one disastrous dinner during which his date had
picked at a salad, complaining the dressing was too
rich to be fat free, then gone on to tell Robert's father he
was crazy to eat red meat these days. "One who is gentle of heart, but has blisters on her hands," his mother
had counseled, "who isn't afraid to laugh instead of tit-
ter. A lady who can occasionally be unladylike."

*One whose eyes are the most amazing shade of green,
who's completely inept at hiding whatever she's feeling at a
particular moment.* Ruthie would be a lousy poker
player, he realized. Then again, Robert had never really cared for poker.

With her zany personality, he imagined she
wouldn't be much of an office person, either. He didn't
know what Ruthie did for a living, but he would bet
his last dollar it had nothing to do with finances, exec-
utives, or business.

He was about to ask her when she slid from her stool
and tried to push her feet into her emerald-green
pumps. "This was the color my dress was supposed to
be," she explained ruefully.

"It would have looked beautiful on you."

She winced as she slipped the other shoe on.
"Shouldn't have taken them off. Now they're killing
me." She leaned against the table and bent forward to
adjust the shoe, giving Robert a clear view of the deep
cleavage revealed by her dress. The fact that he knew

he shouldn't look didn't stop him from staring, nearly choking on a mouthful of air he suddenly felt incapable of drawing into his lungs.

"Time to shuffle off," she said.

"You're staying here in the hotel?" he asked, figuring she was but wanting to get more information from her.

She nodded. "I don't have to, since my apartment's only a few miles away. But I should take advantage of the free room, especially after so much champagne."

Ruthie reached for the green handbag lying on the table. As she pulled the strap of the bag, she wobbled on her high heels, pulling too hard and spilling the bag, and its contents, all over the floor. "Oh, rats," she muttered as she bent over to retrieve her belongings.

Robert froze. She hunched right in front of him, between her vacant stool and his knees, and the images that ran through his brain would have given quite a shock to colleagues who considered him a responsible, conservative man.

She rested one small hand on his thigh to steady herself, refreshing in her complete unselfconsciousness, yet utterly devastating to his composure. He watched, focusing on those fingers pressing into the gray fabric of his slacks. It took her forever, it seemed, to retrieve her comb, lipstick, room key and a bundle of netting filled with birdseed.

Robert's mouth felt like it contained a cup of sawdust. He couldn't swallow. Couldn't breathe without thinking about it. He had the most intense longing to watch her hand move higher, stroking his leg, pulling him down to kneel on the floor with her. Or better yet, to bring her to her feet, then lower her onto the top of the sturdy, butcher-block table. The memory of the pale skin of her thighs above the lace of her white stockings returned with gut-clenching intensity.

Get real, Robert! You've known the woman an hour!

She was vulnerable, depressed, and had consumed more champagne than she should have. No way would he take advantage, even if the sparkle in her eye while they'd talked had told him, without words, she was attracted to him, too.

No. Tonight would be about chocolate cake and laughter and champagne. His hands on her body, her lips on his mouth, her scent filling his head and her sighs of pleasure would all come another night. *No question about it.*

"Yours, I believe?" she said as she pulled herself up, still using his knee for leverage. He didn't know what she meant until she dropped the condom on the table with a smirk. "Even though you say you don't need it, I don't suppose we ought to leave it here on the floor for the staff to find!"

He shook his head. "Maybe not." He glanced down. "See the other room key down there anywhere?"

He didn't spot it right away, but Ruthie apparently did. She pointed to the foot of the table. "Right there. I would offer to get it, but I'm wobbly enough on these stupid shoes and don't think I could manage bending over again! Although, I don't have to worry about being embarrassed if I fall on my fanny right in front of you, do I? I mean, you've already pretty much seen me at my worst."

"This is your worst? Piece of cake!"

They both looked over at the remains of the decimated chocolate cake resting on the table and laughed in unison.

Sliding off his stool, Robert stooped down to retrieve

the key, not even thinking about how close she stood. He found himself practically kneeling at her feet, his face level with her right hip. His mouth was close to her body, close enough that he could see her dress ruffle with his every exhalation. He swallowed hard.

As if he wasn't distracted enough by the sight of her hip and the tempting curve of her sweet backside just inches from his face, she chose that moment to turn toward him. "Having trouble?" she asked, leaning over to look down at him.

He stifled a groan. Oh, yeah, he was having some serious trouble. Trouble breathing. Trouble swallowing. Trouble thinking about anything except that she now stood directly in front of him and if he leaned forward he could press a hot kiss onto her stomach. Elsewhere. Everywhere.

She'd taste sweet—*chocolate and champagne* and the joy that was the essence of her.

"Do you need help?"

He definitely needed her help. But not now, not this soon, not with her in mourning for a newly ended relationship with another man. At least, he *hoped* it was ended.

Tomorrow, however, was another story. He'd camp out in the lobby of the hotel, if he had to, to find out who she was and where she lived. Suddenly, the upcoming months filled with business trips to Philadelphia seemed much more appealing.

"Did you find your key or not? I could have sworn I saw it there by the table leg," she said, her tone concerned.

The key. Monica's room key. He felt it with the tips of his fingers and quickly palmed it. Still kneeling, he slowly shifted his gaze upward, until his eyes met hers and locked. He knew his expression revealed too much of what was going on in his head and the rest of his body. There was no hiding it. There would *definitely* be no hiding it when he stood up, considering the uncomfortable tightness in his trousers.

She understood. Her cheeks suddenly suffused with color. Her mouth fell open as she pulled in a deep breath. He heard the rustling of her dress as she moved her legs close together and Robert had to close his eyes to shake the image of her clenching those pale thighs.

He rose to his feet slowly, as if someone was pushing down on his shoulders from above. They stood, toe to toe, and he marveled at how petite she was, the top of her head only reaching his nose, even though she wore high heels.

"Meet me for breakfast," he urged, trying to find something to say, something else to do with his mouth so he wouldn't give in to the urge to lean forward and lick the chocolate off her lips.

She hesitated, biting the corner of her mouth. "I have a meeting here in the hotel in the morning."

"Lunch then. Better yet, why don't you meet me back here tomorrow night at midnight? I've heard this place serves a pretty wicked cheesecake."

"They do," she said with a tiny smile. "But I don't think that's such a good idea."

"Why not?"

He watched regret cross her features as she took a step back, pulling her pocketbook up to her chest as if using it as a shield. "Look, I said a lot of things tonight, things I should never have said to a stranger. I'm not normally like this. Tonight was brought on by champagne and a good heaping helping of self-pity. But tomorrow, when I remember all of this, *if* I remember all of this, I'm going to feel like an idiot."

"So we can both feel like idiots together."

She shook her head. "If you see me tomorrow, if we bump into each other in the elevator, please pretend to-night never happened, let me think I imagined or dreamed it all, because it would be too humiliating to know it was true."

He could see by the determined set of her chin that she meant it. Of course, there was no way Robert was going to let that happen. But there was no point argu-ing about it tonight. She'd find out soon enough that when he found something he truly wanted, he could be relentless in pursuit of it.

And now he very much wanted *her*.

RUTHIE LEFT HER dream man at the entrance to the res-taurant. He went one way, toward the elevator, and she headed toward the lobby. Part of her was relieved he'd agreed to forget tonight had ever happened. An-other part was sad she'd ever asked him to. She had a feeling it was just as well she didn't know his name. He'd never mentioned it, and she'd never thought to ask. If she had, she might have been tempted to peek at the registration records for his room number. "No, Sin-clair. You're swearing off men starting right now," she muttered as she rounded the corner next to the front desk.

"Swearing off men?"

Ruthie glared at her cousin, Chuck, who'd obviously heard her comment. Chuck, Celeste and Denise's only brother, worked as the night front desk manager. He'd left the wedding shortly before Ruthie had, so she didn't ask him what happened after she'd slipped out. "Yes. You're all a bunch of heartbreakers!"

"Guess ya didn't have such a great time at Celeste's wedding, huh?" Chuck replied. A goofy grin creased his face and he suddenly looked like the surfer dude he wanted to be. Chuck didn't exactly match the hotel's clean-cut image, with his shoulder-length, bleach-blond hair, tanned complexion, and perpetual lazy grin. "So'dja catch the flower thing or what? I had to leave early and didn't see that part."

"No, I didn't catch the bouquet. Thank goodness."

He shrugged. "I thought you old single chicks dug that, you know, getting your hopes up and all."

Ruthie leaned across the three-foot-wide expanse of polished oak that made up the front check-in desk and grabbed a fistful of her cousin's shirt. "Old? You think I'm old?"

He grimaced and held his hands up protectively. "Nah, not old. I mean, it's not like you're pushin' *thirty* or anything!"

"You're on a roll now, Chuckie," she snarled. "Why don't you dig yourself in deeper?"

He suddenly looked shocked. "Oh, man, Ruthie, you're thirty? When did that happen?"

Ruthie sighed in exasperation. "Chuck, sweetie, remember when you were *six* and you ruined my *twelfth* birthday slumber party because you kept coming to the door of my room and trying to throw spitballs at my friends? And I told you I was going to make you eat *six* of them, one for *each* year I'd had to suffer with you on the planet?"

The head bobbed, slowly. A grin creased his face. "Yeah, and I hit Denise in her head and she ran crying to your mom."

Ruthie had forgotten that. "Okay, so it wasn't *all* bad."

He snorted a laugh. "She sure was ticked. So why'd ya mention that?"

She explained slowly. "I was turning twelve. You were already six. Uh, how old are you now, Chuck?"

He hesitated for a moment longer than anyone should have when asked that question. "Twenty-three next month."

She waited, watching the wheels churn behind the bright blue eyes. Saw him calculate. "Oh, yeah, right," he finally said with the lazy nod. "See, I toldja I didn't miss it."

"There's a reason you're so gorgeous," Ruthie muttered beneath her breath. Her mother's favorite saying suddenly popped into her head. *Heaven distributes its gifts.*

Chuck got the tall, blond, lean and gorgeous genes. He was like Ruthie's late father and her uncle in that respect—and like Celeste and Denise. But Chuck had been just a bit shortchanged in the "quick" department. "I guess there are worse things than big hips and kinky red hair," she continued with a yawn.

"Huh?"

"Never mind, sweetie," she said as she wearily turned toward the elevator. "I was just coming in to say good-night. I'm going up to my room. Don't call me in the morning, as I'm quite sure I'll be sleeping off a champagne headache."

He smirked. "Yeah, I'll bet. You must've had a hellish good time. I've never seen you rockin' when you're walkin'."

She didn't ask what he meant, too tired to try to follow his reasoning tonight. "The ceremony was beautiful," she conceded. "But I'd rather forget everything else that happened this evening."

"That bad?"

A flash of memory brought a sudden warmth to her cheeks. The man. The dark-haired stranger in the kitchen. Well, she might want to forget how foolish she must have appeared to him, but she certainly would never forget the expression on his face—the one that said he thought she was desirable.

But she'd never see him again. Which was what she'd wanted, wasn't it? Even if it wasn't, it didn't matter. She never got his name! She'd never asked, probably subconsciously keeping their interlude anonymous, enjoying its mystery and magic.

"Let's just say, after I watched Celeste tie the knot, the evening went downhill faster than *you* did the time you broke your arm trying to sled on a greased trash can lid."

He looked puzzled, trying to place the memory. Ruthie blew him a tired kiss and turned to leave the lobby.

"Hey, Ruthie, take a few aspirin tonight before you go to sleep. Should make you feel better in the a.m."

She gave a rueful chuckle. "Chuck, there is absolutely nothing that can happen to me tonight that will make me feel better in the a.m."

3

TO HER DISMAY, Ruthie realized when she reached her room that her bad-awful day was not over yet. Staring dumbly at the doorknob, which remained stiff and unmoving in her hand, she jammed the key in once more. "Stupid old locks!"

It didn't help. The room key would not open the door. "Great, oh, just great," she muttered, tired and wanting nothing more than to kick off her too-tight shoes and fall into the king-size bed on the other side of the stubborn door.

Wearily making her way down the hall toward the elevator, Ruthie paused to pick up a white courtesy phone residing on a small telephone table. Hoping she wouldn't have to explain to Chuck the intricacies of locks and keys, she nearly cheered when someone else answered in the lobby.

"Tina? Why does Chuck have you working the desk?"

"Smoke break," the other woman said. Ruthie heard a distinct popping sound and knew Tina was cracking bubble gum, probably thick, pink, and shiny. "I'm off at two, so he took a last ten."

Ruthie quickly explained her problem, and asked Tina to send the late-night bellman up to her room with a passkey.

"Well, I dunno," Tina said doubtfully. The gum

snapped again. "We're not supposed to without the manager's okay."

Ruthie clenched her teeth as a sinus and champagne headache pounded in her brain. She sniffed and counted to five. "Tina, you know my voice. You know me. Look in the logs and you'll see I am registered in room four-twelve. And if you ever want to come into my kitchen during your breaks and try to beg me for sweets again you'd better send the bellman up with the key."

At the mention of food, Tina perked right up. "You betcha. It'll cost some key lime pie." She paused. "But, hey, tomorrow's Monday, your night off!"

"Thankfully, yes," Ruthie replied, glad she wouldn't have to spend tomorrow afternoon and evening in the hotel kitchen, pretending everything was peachy keen. "Even we chefs get an occasional day off. Come by later in the week."

A bellman was at Ruthie's door five minutes after she hung up the phone. He was new and didn't know her, thank goodness. He didn't ask why she was locked out of her room, wearing her ugly dress, with bobby pins sticking out of her hair and a pair of emerald-green pumps dangling from the tips of her fingers.

After he unlocked the door, she murmured her thanks, entered the room, and tossed her shoes into a corner. "Sleep," she said with a sigh, eyeing the king-size bed which made the one in her small apartment look like a twin.

Tugging at the zipper on the back of her hated dress, Ruthie carelessly pulled it off and dropped it to the floor. She gave it a kick, then actually walked across it toward her suitcase. As she walked, she caught sight of herself in the floor-length mirror on the door of the bathroom.

"Not bad, Sinclair. Coulda made some man pretty happy tonight," she said with a sigh as she studied herself.

Celeste had wonderful taste in lingerie. Her bridesmaid gift to Ruthie—an ivory-colored silk camisole and tap pants set, with matching thigh-high stockings and a lacy little bra that pushed up more than it held in—did wonderful things for Ruthie's curvy figure. "Not that anyone will ever see it."

Too tired to dig through her suitcase for her plain old Winnie-the-Pooh nightshirt, Ruthie fell onto the bed. Reaching for the bedside table, she flicked off the light and sighed as the room descended into blackness. Her sigh trailed off as she realized something was wrong.

The room was spinning.

She hadn't gone to bed in a spinning room since college. To be precise, since the night in junior year when one of her roommates had told Ruthie she was sick of seeing her drink sissy white wine spritzers and challenged her to match her, shot for shot, with some cheap Mexican tequila.

Ruthie didn't like to lose. So she'd drunk the other girl right under the table. Literally. That night had resulted in a spinning room. Then, when told *she'd* been the one who'd swallowed the worm, the night had also resulted in Ruthie's one and only experience sleeping on a bathroom floor.

Tonight she was not toilet-hugging intoxicated. She was just pleasantly woozy. Remembering a trick she'd once heard about, Ruthie stuck one leg out from under the covers, liking the way the silky stocking slid against the starched fabric of the linens, almost a light caress.

"Pathetic. Now I'm even liking the sheets touching me!"

Wiggling toward the edge of the bed so she could place her foot on the floor, she willed the room to remain still. Badly needing sleep, she ignored the childhood whisper cautioning against letting a solitary leg dangle where monsters underneath the bed could grab it.

The trick helped with the spinniness. But nothing was making the sinus headache go away. It throbbed every time she shifted on the unfamiliar pillow.

"Aspirin," she muttered. Gingerly sliding out of the bed, she staggered to the bathroom. Unwilling to let vicious shards of light pierce her brain, she felt around in the dark, trying to find the aspirin she always carried in her makeup bag. First her fingers found a brand-new box of condoms. She sighed as she remembered stopping at a convenience store near the hotel on her way to the reception. Fully decked out in her atrocious wedding regalia, shopping for prophylactics, she must have made quite a picture for the teenage clerk, who'd winked as she'd paid him.

Finding the bottle of aspirin, Ruthie flipped a couple of pills into her hand. Popping two in her mouth, she turned on the faucet. Her head screamed as she bent to drink straight from the tap. "Maybe one more," she whispered as she straightened. Not able to bend over again, she ignored the fact that it would taste chalky and bitter, popped another pill in her mouth and swallowed it dry.

She was halfway back to the bed, still woozy, headachy and nearly blind in the darkness of the room, when she realized the pill *hadn't* tasted chalky and bitter. Horrified, she turned, ignoring the stab of pain in her skull, and dashed back into the bathroom. She flipped on the light, shuddered at its intensity, and grabbed the still-open bottle on the counter.

"Cold medication," she said. She blinked rapidly to try to clear her eyes enough to read the label. "May cause drowsiness. Alcohol may enhance this effect." Capping the bottle, she tucked it back in her bag, next to the bottle of aspirin, then looked at her reflection in the mirror. "You could give Frankenstein's bride a run for her money," she told herself, noting the wild hair, and the dark smudges of makeup under her eyes. "And now you've gone and drugged yourself but good."

Stupid. Stupid, Sinclair.

But not lethal. She was going to be having a much deeper, and longer, night's sleep than she expected, it seemed. Flipping off the light, she went back into the bedroom, pausing to set the clock on the bedside table. She hadn't bothered earlier, knowing she hadn't slept past nine in years and the board meeting wasn't until eleven. Now, however, it seemed wise to take the precaution!

Reclining on the bed, she was out before she even thought to stick her foot back on the floor.

ROBERT FOUND HIMSELF back in the bar after he left Ruthie at the entrance to the hotel restaurant. He didn't need another drink, heaven knew, but he needed something else: time. Time to figure out how to handle the Monica situation.

"Honesty. Tonight. Get it out in the open so she can get whatever fit she's gonna throw off her chest before tomorrow morning's board meeting," he told himself as he took one last sip of his champagne. Somehow, after leaving Ruthie in the kitchen, he didn't have the heart to return to vodka tonics.

The waiter gave him a confused look as he heard him mumbling to himself, but smiled in appreciation when he saw the big tip Robert left on the table. "Honesty's the best policy," the waiter said with a grin. "Honesty...and generosity!"

Leaving the bar, Robert pulled Monica's key from his pocket and headed to the elevator. He glanced at the room number on the tab. "Four-twelve." He entered the elevator and punched the fourth-floor button. "Okay, Monica, show time."

When he got upstairs, he walked slowly down the silent corridor, wondering why his feet suddenly felt leaden. "Just get it over with," he told himself. "In and out." The thought struck a raw chord in his mind and he grimaced. "No, not in and out! Just there and gone."

When he reached four-twelve, he knocked quietly. No answer. He knocked again, louder, hoping the occupants in the nearby rooms were not light sleepers. "Come on, Monica, I know you're awake," he growled at the closed door.

She was taking this too far, forcing him to use the key. A big part of him was tempted to forget about it, deal with her histrionics in the morning when he had a clear head. But he wanted it done. For some odd reason, though he wasn't even involved with Monica Winchester, he felt the need to get this situation resolved before he set out to find—and seduce—the red-haired angel he'd met two hours before in the kitchen.

Against his better judgment, he slipped the key into the lock and pushed into the darkened room. Darkened wasn't quite the right adjective. The place was nearly pitch-black and he had to stand in the doorway to let his eyes adjust. Glancing over his shoulder, he saw the elevator doors slide open, so he quickly entered and shut the door behind him. "Monica?" he whispered, his voice painfully loud in the silence.

A mumbling sound emanated from the left side of the room, and Robert was finally able to make out what appeared to be a bed. A very large bed. "Who...?" the woman said.

"It's Robert," he said, stepping closer. Asleep? She'd fallen asleep? Though relieved that she was obviously not expecting him to show up, his masculine pride took a hit.

"Bobby?" she said, her voice muffled, heavy with sleep and grogginess. "You came. You used the key."

Bobby? No one had ever called him that—a miracle, given his southern upbringing. He didn't like it. "Yes, but not for the reason you think," he said as he crossed to the bed. He set the key on the bedside table. "I'll leave this here, and we'll forget about this whole thing."

She whimpered. "No."

Something, the pleading sound? The raw need? Something in her voice, in that single word, made him stop from turning around and leaving the room. "Are you all right?"

"I don't want to be alone," she murmured on a sigh. "I'm so tired of being alone."

Something wasn't right. As far as he knew, Monica Winchester had spent very few nights alone in her adult life. Curious, he leaned closer and caught a whiff of two sweet, unmistakable scents. Chocolate. And champagne.

RUTHIE WAS IN the midst of a lovely dream. Somehow, in the strange way dreams have of seeming so real, she imagined he really had come into her room. *It's Robert*, he'd said. How quaint of Bobby to use his full name, she'd thought dreamily. But the fantasy quickly shifted.

She didn't want him to come to her. Not anymore. It wasn't Bobby she wanted in her room, and as she floated along, experiencing the strangely real scene, she pictured another man. The dark-haired man from the kitchen. The one with the eyes that devoured her and the lips she'd wanted to taste from the moment she'd seen them. The one who'd laughed with her, teased her, listened to her silliness and made her wish they'd met under different circumstances.

Though no one was supposed to have control over her dreams, for some reason, Ruthie did, for suddenly the man standing beside her bed, talking to her, *was* the man from the kitchen.

"Better," she murmured, and she smiled.

"Ruthie?" the dream man asked, with perhaps more surprise than she'd expect from a fantasy lover.

She sighed, twisted and kicked at the covers which had become too hot, too confining, wanting to free her body of their cumbersome weight. She heard him groan, her fantasy man, then somehow saw him reach to tug apart the curtains at the nearby window to bathe the room in the gentle glow of the full moon.

"Oh, God, Ruthie," he said, this time his voice taut and hoarse, full of something—a sound she was unfamiliar with, but could identify as need, desire. That was better. Now he sounded the way any dream lover should sound. Like he couldn't get enough of her, though he hadn't even touched her yet.

But he would. Oh yes, the night was long, and her dreams promised to be rich...and fulfilling.

EVERY OUNCE of decency in Robert Kendall's being urged him to turn around, leave the key on the table, and lock the door behind him. Every lesson his mama had taught him about how to be a gentleman screamed at him. *She called him Bobby, probably her boyfriend's name! She didn't know who he was. She was obviously suffering the effects of too much champagne and a stressful night. Get the hell out now!*

But, louse that he was, he couldn't make himself walk away.

"You're beautiful," he murmured hoarsely, almost wishing he hadn't pulled aside the curtain. With her pale body bathed in the golden glow of moonlight, she was too damned tempting.

She was dressed for seduction, for pleasure. The ivory satin lingerie she wore clung to the ripe curves of her body, hugging her hips, caught coyly between her pale thighs. Those legs—still encased in the white stockings—were not hard, not muscular, not firm. They were soft, rounded, meant to be touched and stroked. Kissed. He couldn't tear his gaze away.

Until he noticed the thinness of her silky camisole. It had slipped down, revealing only the tiniest, most minuscule bit of lacy bra he'd ever seen. It was too small, made for a less endowed woman, and Ruthie's lush breasts nearly spilled free of it. Even in the shadows he saw the dusky highlight of her nipples, not even an inch below the top of the lace, and his mouth went dry, his breathing became labored.

"Ruthie," he muttered, trying to find the will to turn away, "I'm not who you think I am."

"You are," she whispered. "You are, and you came, and I'm so glad."

Before he knew what was happening, she'd reached up, sliding her hand over his shoulder, tugging him down until he toppled onto the bed, on top of her. Then she was kissing him, and oh, sweet heaven, her mouth, her lovely, smiling mouth, that had driven him mad from the moment he'd seen her licking the chocolate icing off her fork, made him forget everything but sensation. She nibbled, slid her lips on his, licked hungrily at him until he couldn't restrain himself and drew her entire body up tightly against his, so he could deepen the kiss. Then he was drowning in her, lost in her taste and smell, the champagne, the chocolate, the essence of her sweetness.

He moved lower, dropping kisses below her jaw, to the softness of her neck, the tender spot at the base of her ear. She writhed gently against him, pressing her silk-clad body even closer.

"I am so glad you found me," she whispered as he placed a kiss at the base of her throat. "I didn't want to be alone."

She didn't want to be alone. So she'd invited another man to spend the night with her.

The realization shocked him back into reality, forcing Robert to pull away. She sighed in disappointment, reaching for him again. Giving his head a few hard shakes, Robert struggled to slow his ragged breathing, tried to control his body's reaction to her embrace. "Ruthie, this isn't right. I'm not the one you want."

In the soft light, he saw that, though her eyes remained closed, a smile crossed her face. "Of course you're the one I want. Especially now."

"Why now?" he asked, curious about this odd conversation he was having with a woman who was practically asleep.

"Now that I know we have *more* than *chocolate*."

Her words hit him hard, like individual bolts of lightning. They struck, sunk in, hit home. *She knew who he was.*

Robert felt like chortling with glee.

It made sense. She'd been no more than tipsy downstairs an hour ago. Her mood now was obviously languorous, seductive, not groggy as he'd first thought.

Robert had never made love to a stranger. But, though he'd known her only a few hours, this woman didn't seem like a stranger to him. It was meant to be, from their surrealistic meeting in the kitchen, to the instant recognition and strong attraction they'd felt for one another. Even the obvious mix-up with the room keys. Whatever whim of fate or chance had brought them together, he could only give thanks for it and was not going to second-guess it. And, he'd be willing to bet, he'd live the rest of his life without ever regretting this night.

"You really want me, Ruthie? Because if you say yes, I'm going to be here until tomorrow morning, and I can guarantee you, you won't be getting a restful night's sleep."

She chuckled, a throaty, earthy sound that rolled over his body, making his skin feel too tight against his own muscles. "If my dreams are like this, who needs a restful sleep?"

This time when she reached for him he didn't pull away. Following her down onto the bed, he found her mouth again and kissed her, sensing her complete lack of inhibition as she caught his tongue in a slow dance with her own. Her hands lazily moved across his shoulders, pushing off his jacket, and he helped her, shrugging free of it and tossing it to the floor.

"Still not right," she murmured as she pulled at his shirt.

"Let me." He gently brushed her hands aside to undo a few buttons. Unwilling to waste time with them all, he unfastened the wrists, then yanked the shirt over his head.

Her small hands were cool, pale, as soft as the rest of her. They roamed over the flatness of his chest with a touch as light and fleeting as the brush of a feather. After his experiences with women who demanded, who twisted and thrust and writhed, Robert found himself completely overwhelmed. The gentle look of wonder on Ruthie's face as she used her fingers to trail a path through his chest hair made him ache, and he wanted to do the same thing to her.

His hands nearly shook as he slid them over her body. Slick, no friction from the silky lingerie. Her skin was just as smooth. When he moved his palm beneath the lower hem of the camisole to caress her soft, bare belly, he was startled at the vibrant warmth. She looked so pale, so ethereal in the moonlight, but her flesh was hot, trembling.

She moaned. "I want your hands all over me."

"Here?" he whispered against her neck, moving his palms until they rested right below the tiny lace bra. He slid a finger up, scraping the pebble-hard nipple through the lace. "Here?"

"Yes. Please, yes."

She didn't have to ask him twice. He lifted himself up enough to push the camisole up. She helped him, wiggling and pulling the fabric over her head, across the mass of red curls on the pillow. Robert watched her every move, every wriggle, unable to look away.

Reaching for the front clasp of the bra, which strained to hold in her breasts, he deftly undid it. He was unable to withhold a smile of male satisfaction as he watched her breasts fall free, right into his palms. She moaned when he slid his hands over them, catching her nipples between his fingers.

Unable to wait, he lowered his head, replacing fingers with lips as he sucked her flesh into his mouth. This time she hissed. Her hips bucked in reaction. "You like that," he whispered. She didn't reply immediately, merely arched up into him.

"More," she whispered, reaching down to the waistband of his trousers. He followed her lead, undoing the slacks, letting her push them from his hips. She made a sigh of disappointment when he had to stand up next to the bed to quickly remove the last of his clothes. For the first time tonight, he had reason to be thankful to Monica, and he reached into his jacket pocket for the condom she'd provided.

Ruthie didn't give him a chance to open the thing before she rolled onto her side, reaching out to caress his bare hip. Her eyes opened lazily. "Oh, my." She stared at his erection, nibbling at the corner of her lip. A smile curled across her face. "I've never dreamed of quite so...much before."

Chuckling, Robert pulled the condom on, knowing she was watching. Seeing the tightness of her nipples and the restless shifting of her thighs, he could see she paid very careful attention.

Lowering his hand to her leg, he smiled when she arched her hips, silently inviting him to touch her higher. And he did, after he first pulled off the damp tap pants. He nearly groaned when he slipped his finger into the hot, wet curls at the apex of her thighs.

"I want to do so much with you," he muttered hoarsely as he bent to catch her mouth in another deep kiss.

She moved beneath him, parting her legs, wrapping her dimpled softness around his own limbs until he was positioned at the entrance to her body. "We have all night," she said with a sultry smile. "This dream can go on all night long."

Needing no further cajoling, Robert slid into her, slowly, liking her tightness and her heat, liking how she swallowed him up until he couldn't tell whether he was feeling her body or his own. "All night long," he reminded her as he matched the rhythm of her gently rotating hips.

RUTHIE'S EROTIC DREAMS went on and on and on. She'd never, in real life, made love with such complete lack of inhibition. In the few sexual encounters she'd had before, there had been the concerns: Were her hips too wide? Did he love her? Was that all there was to it—where was the explosion?

But in last night's long surreal fantasy, she experienced perfection. Not once. Not twice. Somehow, the amazing dream had included making love with her beautiful stranger three times. The third had her climbing up on top of him, allowing her too-large breasts to fall freely near his face, something she would have been much too self-conscious to do in real life! But her dream man had loved it. He'd kept leaning up to kiss and lick and suckle, finally holding her hips steady while he thrust up into her over and over again until she experienced an earth-shaking orgasm and collapsed on top of him.

Could she really have climaxed in her sleep? She wondered about it in the morning as the intrusive light of the sun slid between the open curtains into her hotel room. She thought she'd closed them the night before, but given her befuddled state, and the medication, she could have been wrong.

Snuggling deeper under the covers, she surreptitiously opened one eye and glanced at the bedside clock. Early. Only eight o'clock. Why was she awake? She closed her eye, wanting to return to her dream, wanting to lose herself in the erotic imaginary world in which she'd spent the previous night.

That was when she heard the water running in the bathroom.

"What on earth?" she said aloud as she sat straight up in bed, letting the sheets fall into a pile on her lap. The artificially cooled air of the room struck her, and she looked down, stupidly wondering what had happened to her clothes, as she was completely naked!

Before she could even begin to form an explanation in her mind, the bathroom door opened.

And she screamed.

4

HEARING RUTHIE SCREAM, Robert assumed the worst—someone was trying to break in. Ignoring the fact that he was completely naked, he raced out of the bathroom and spun toward the door, assuming a defensive crouch.

The door was shut tight. Good thing, he realized, because given his position, and lack of clothing, he would have provided one hell of a vulnerable target to any intruder.

"Ruthie, what's wrong?" he asked as he turned around.

She sat on the bed, wearing nothing but her thick red hair, her face a mask of absolute horror and shock. "You. It's you."

"What's me?"

Her mouth fell open as she let her stare travel from the top of his head all the way down his body. Her eyes widened and he could see her gulp as she paused to gaze longer at certain parts of his anatomy. Her face turned a charming shade of pink which didn't at all clash with her bright red curls. The parts she was staring at reacted quickly. Not surprising, since he didn't think he could ever get enough of her. Their night had been one long sensual fantasy.

Her mouth opened even more, wide enough that she could probably have shoved her fist into it, as he hardened before her eyes. His soft laughter drew her attention to his face. Their eyes met and locked, his reflecting the heat he knew was burning him from the inside out. Hers looking...horrified. "Ruth?"

She shook her head, bemused. The movement caused her red curls to fall over her shoulders, curtaining her breasts. Peeking between the tresses were the pink nipples he'd been kissing just a few hours before. She was a beautiful picture in the morning light. Sleepy. Tousled. Like a woman who'd been thoroughly made love to for hours. Which she had.

As if she'd suddenly realized what he was staring at, she grabbed at the sheets and yanked them up to her chin. "What are you doing? What is going on here?"

Ruthie shook her head again, trying to make it function. Was she still asleep? she wondered. Was this part of her dream?

How could the man from the kitchen be in her room?

"I didn't mean to wake you. I needed to clean up so I could kiss you good morning," he said with a boyish grin. Like a playful lover.

Lover? "Oh, my God."

"No regrets in the morning light, Ruthie," he said, making a *tsk*ing sound.

"Exactly how much do I have to regret?" she whispered.

"Nothing," he replied. "It was fate. The room keys getting mixed up, us having this instant—I don't know what to call it—attraction doesn't seem enough. Is *connection* too strong a word?"

The keys had gotten mixed up. And she'd been lethargic and woozy from champagne, nearly knocked out by the cold medicine.

It had happened. It had been real. She groaned and

threw herself back onto the pillow, willing herself to wake up from what she so wished was a nightmare!

He walked toward her, completely unselfconscious in his nakedness. Unable to resist, she turned her head and peeked again at the perfect lines of his body. Smooth, muscular, lean and hard. She rubbed the tips of her fingers together, still able to feel the taut flesh of his back and thighs, the wiry dark hair on his chest.

"More?" he said as he caught her looking.

Ruthie felt a hot blush rise into her cheeks as she quickly turned her attention to her own clenched fingers.

Chuckling, he sat next to her on the bed. He gently stroked her shoulder, brushing her hair away from her face with infinite tenderness. "You're blushing," he said, amusement lacing his tone. "You can't be embarrassed around me, can you? Please, don't be, Ruthie. Last night was beyond anything I've ever experienced."

She heard the sincerity and tenderness in his voice, saw a smile of recollection on his face, and wished she could join in on the shared memory. A collage of dreamy images swirled in her brain. Visions of caresses, kisses, his hands, his lips. Her fingernails digging into him. Their mouths on each other's... "Oh, no!" she said aloud, wondering if she'd truly experienced oral sex for the first time and could barely remember it.

"Are you okay?" he said as he lifted the covers and slid into bed next to her.

Ruthie shot to the other side of the king-size bed so fast she nearly fell face-first out onto the floor. "Um...I think we need to talk," she croaked out as she stood up, tugging the sheet with her. She wrapped it around herself, sarong style, then breathed deeply for courage before looking back at the dark-haired stranger she'd made love with all night long.

He reclined on the bed, resting his head back on his crossed arms. A five o'clock shadow heightened the lines of his jaw, enhancing the sex appeal he so easily exuded. His chest was bare, the bottom half of his body covered only by a dark green blanket. Ruthie felt like she was looking at a picture right out of a woman's fantasy magazine. She'd been with this man? She, Ruthie Sinclair, had *had* this man? And she'd been barely conscious enough to remember any of the details? She sighed. "Sometimes life is just too unfair."

A wicked expression crossed his face. "You didn't think we played fair? As I recall, the score is four to three."

Not knowing what he was talking about, she shook her head, which still felt stuffed with cotton. "Four to three?"

He nodded. "That last time for you was definitely a multiple."

Understanding, Ruthie groaned and pulled the sheet up until it completely covered her head, knowing she probably looked like a kid in a homemade ghost costume. "Please just go away."

"What?" he asked.

Ruthie mumbled the request again. When she heard the bed creak, she mentally crossed her fingers that he was going to do as she asked. The firm tugging of the sheet from her clenched hands told her that wish wasn't going to be granted. She caught the sheet before it could fall too far, and clenched it right above her breasts.

"Ruthie, please, tell me what's the matter."

Knowing she was going to have to tell him the truth, as farfetched as it might sound, Ruthie took a deep breath. "Okay, we need to talk. Here's what happened, uh...oh, good heavens, I don't even know your name!"

Tears welled up in Ruthie's eyes and she threw herself face-first onto the bed. A moment ago she would not have believed things could actually be any worse, but she now realized they were. *She didn't know his name.* She had just had a one-night stand with a nameless stranger! She'd done it. Ruthie Sinclair had officially crossed the ranks and become a "bad girl."

"I'm a tramp. You might as well call the *Jerry Springer Show* and tell them I'm on my way," she wailed into the pillow.

She heard his chuckle and felt the bed sink as he sat down.

"My name is Robert. Robert Kendall," he whispered. She felt his breath as he spoke, because his mouth was mere inches from the soft flesh at the back of her knee. Then his lips touched her there, gently, tenderly. No one had ever kissed that spot on her before, and Ruthie was shocked at the waves of pleasure that washed up from her legs into her lower body. Before she even thought to move away, she felt his hand slide up the back of her bare thigh and tenderly cup her buttocks, with all the familiarity of a longtime lover.

"Hands off, mister!" she snarled as she rolled over to the far edge of the bed. "Don't touch me."

Seeing the downright misery on Ruthie's face finally broke through Robert's sleepy, muddled brain. She wasn't playing, wasn't being coy as he'd thought a few minutes earlier when she'd so adorably tugged the sheet over her head. There was something seriously wrong. Backing off the bed, he glanced around the floor and saw his trousers. Tugging them on, he walked over and sat down in a chair close to the door. "Okay, talk to me. Tell me what's going on here."

She stared at him, biting her lip uncertainly. Her pink tongue slid out to moisten her lips and Robert felt a sudden rush of lust as he remembered how she'd tasted...and how she'd tasted him.

"Last night, uh, you came into my room because our keys got mixed up, right? I can't really understand that. I mean, didn't you know your own room number?"

Robert didn't think Ruthie would appreciate hearing the whole Monica story. He gave her an abbreviated version, leaving out certain details. Like the part about Monica giving him the condom and asking him to spend the night with her. It would be too easy for Ruthie to imagine he'd gone to Monica's room to do just that, and exchanged one warm willing body for another!

"So, you needed to meet with your business associate in the middle of the night, and let yourself into his room with a key?" she asked after he'd finished.

"Something like that," Robert said. "And after I got in the room I realized my mistake."

"But you stayed anyway," she said, her voice loaded with accusation. "Knowing I was asleep you...you..."

"Hold it right there," he said, lifting his hands, palms out. "*You* kissed *me!* And then you made it very obvious you knew *who* I was and *what* you wanted."

"So you just climbed on in," she said.

He couldn't stop a wicked chuckle at her words. Ruthie glared, grabbed a pillow from the bed and threw it at him from across the room. "I meant you climbed on into the bed of a complete stranger!"

She had him there. Robert ran a weary hand over his eyes, wondering if he could possibly explain to her what the previous night had meant to him. How she'd freed something in him, some emotion—joy, perhaps?—that he'd kept tightly locked away for a very long time in his quest to succeed. The years of living alone in New York, working eleven or twelve-hour days, having little to no personal life—and thinking he *liked* living that way—had simply disappeared under the powerful force of her smile.

Robert couldn't put it into words. Hell, he could barely understand it himself. All he knew was from the moment he'd stumbled into the kitchen the night before, he'd had a grin on his face and had wanted nothing more than to be with Ruthie.

And after they'd made love... Well, now he didn't know if he was *ever* going to be able to let her go.

"Yes, I did. But Ruthie, I didn't feel like we were strangers. Like I said before, you and I connected last night." Robert watched as she twirled a strand of her hair around her index finger. Obviously a nervous habit. "You felt it too or you wouldn't have asked me to stay and make love to you."

Ruthie shifted on the bed, twisting her hands into the covers and dropping her head forward. He almost didn't hear what she said. "I was asleep. I didn't know what I was doing and if I'd been in my right mind, I *never* would have done it!"

Asleep? Robert stared at her, looking for a shaking of her shoulders that would tell him she was laughing, or joking. There was none. She wouldn't look up at him, wouldn't meet his eyes. Instead of the whimsical charmer he'd met last night, he saw a woman full of self-recrimination and doubt.

Sharp disappointment made his voice scornful. "Well, honey, you obviously woke up. You were definitely a willing participant."

Standing up, Robert grabbed his shirt, jacket and tie off the floor. He was tempted to walk out, carrying the rest of his clothes and shoes, but could only imagine the sight that would make. Especially if a member of the Sinclair family happened to pass him in the hall! Instead, he strode into the bathroom and slammed the door behind him.

Damn! Robert nearly tore his rumpled white dress shirt as he pulled it on, mentally cursing all the while. He couldn't remember the last time he'd felt such a sudden sense of loss.

He'd known Ruthie for less than twelve hours, but the realization that he'd so misjudged her was difficult to swallow. Maybe he'd been so attracted to her physically he'd imagined her joyful, honest spirit. He'd thought he'd seen something in Ruthie that he'd been looking for, perhaps unknowingly, in every woman he'd dated.

He'd believed she was so different, so unique, so charmingly honest. He'd imagined she was able to indulge in pleasure, whether it was eating rich chocolate, drinking intoxicating champagne, or indulging in sensuous lovemaking, without games or apologies.

That morning, he'd even found himself imagining what kind of relationship they could have together. In spite of the obstacles, he'd discovered he wanted just that. Not storybook stuff—white chapel and two-point-five kids—but a passionate, joyful, emotionally fulfilling partnership with a woman who enthralled him like no other one ever had. With no pretense, no demands or false promises for forever, which most women wanted and many men supplied without ever meaning a word.

Robert prided himself on never having done that, at least. Every woman he'd been involved with had known his stand on marriage and family. Those restraints were fine for other people—like his brothers— but not for him. He had no room for them. He'd worked too hard for too many years to move beyond the confines of his childhood.

During that childhood, all his brothers had talked about was working in the business, marrying the girl next door, and breeding lots more Kendalls. They'd liked the noise and confusion and security that came with living in a house with so many other people you couldn't find a moment's privacy unless you locked yourself in a closet.

Robert hadn't. All he'd dreamed about was getting away, being alone. The thought of quiet and solitude to think or study without being interrupted every minute—by a fight breaking out between two brothers in one room, or by another brother sneaking up behind him to do wet willies in his ear—had been pure heaven.

That was why he'd left home, gone to an out-of-state college and never considered going back. He lived alone and had no intention of changing that for anyone—not his parents, nor his siblings. Certainly not for any woman who wanted to fill his quiet, ordered world with lots of loud little kids who'd make his adult life as crowded as his childhood had been.

That wasn't to say he didn't love his family—or wasn't thankful for his warm, supportive upbringing. There was nothing he wouldn't do for his parents or his brothers. Except, of course, move back within a fifty-mile radius of them!

Robert splashed some cold water on his face, rubbed a hand against his unshaven jaw, and tried to imagine what his brothers would say about his current situation. He imagined they'd be laughing like loons considering the lectures he'd given them about sex during their high-school years.

He tried to remember if he'd ever done something as crazy as having a one-night stand with a stranger before last night. No. He knew he hadn't. His last sexual relationship had been with a buyer from Macy's whom he'd dated for a few months, at least until she started hinting about things like closet space and toilet seats left up. That had ended that relationship. He'd been basically celibate ever since. His life was organized, but hectic, revolving around long work hours, some time spent with friends.

He liked it that way, liked working late without having to worry about calling someone to apologize for missing dinner. He enjoyed the fine things his successful career enabled him to buy. He liked physical pleasures: good food, good wine, sex that left him shaken and spent. And he'd thought last night that he'd finally found someone else who liked the same things, with the same sense of abandon. Ruthie.

Then again, maybe being confronted with Monica's calculating, threatening proposal the night before had left him wanting to see genuine honesty of emotion in someone else. He thought he'd seen it in Ruthie. But he was wrong. Now, in the bright light of day, she regretted their lovemaking and was trying to come up with excuses for her behavior. Like so many other people he knew, it appeared Ruthie didn't have the guts to take responsibility for her own actions.

The disappointment tasted so bitter and acrid in his mouth, Robert felt physically ill.

Fully dressed, Robert reached for the doorknob just as he heard a soft knock. He yanked the door open, startling Ruthie, who stood on the other side wearing a long sleepshirt with a big picture of Winnie-the-Pooh.

"Not into tap pants and stockings in the light of day, huh?" he said as he walked past her, ready to leave the room.

"Robert, you said your name's Robert? Please, give me a minute to explain."

He paused, hearing something in her voice, not only self-recrimination, but now, apparently, serious regret.

Taking a deep breath, Robert turned to face her. "Look, Ruth, it's obvious that you have had some second thoughts about what happened between us last night. Yeah, it happened too fast, and we don't know each other. But for you to come up with some b.s. about being asleep is damned cowardly."

"Maybe asleep wasn't the right word," she muttered. "More like drugged."

"Drugged?" he bellowed. "Are you accusing me of slipping you a mickey?"

"No, no," she hurried to explain, grabbing his arm as he again turned to leave. "Not exactly drugged. Intoxicated?"

"Don't even try to say you were drunk, unless you had a fifth of whiskey stashed up here in your room and had one hell of a nightcap after you left the kitchen. You weren't drunk!"

She sighed, took a deep breath, and dropped his arm. "Please, wait here a minute."

Ruthie walked into the bathroom and came back carrying a small bottle, which she pressed into his hand.

"How'd you guess I'm developing a serious headache?"

"Read it."

"Sinus medication. So?"

"So," Ruthie said, "I thought they were aspirin. And when I came up to the room last night, I popped a few of them."

Robert frowned. "You shouldn't take this stuff when you've been drinking."

"My, you're quick on the uptake," she muttered.

She raised a shaky hand to her face, but not before he saw bright tears in her eyes. "Ruthie? Are you telling me this medication made you..."

Her whisper was so soft he nearly didn't hear it. "I thought I was dreaming. I thought it was one long, lovely dream."

Robert dropped the bottle. She really had been asleep? It didn't seem possible. "You were so...enthusiastic!" Her face reddened until the color of her cheeks almost matched her hair. "I'm sorry, I didn't mean to embarrass you. But, hell, Ruthie, you talked to me. And I mean talking, not just moaning and screaming!"

Her face went a shade or two redder. "Please..."

Robert thrust both of his hands into his hair, then pressed his fingers into his temples. "You weren't aware of any of it? I mean, you had no idea what was going on between us?"

"I knew what was happening—I just thought I was dreaming about it happening. Please, Robert, please tell me I'm right in thinking we used protection!"

Seeing the sudden look of panic in her eyes, he nodded. "Yeah. I provided it the first time. Then you told me where to find the box of condoms in your makeup bag."

Knowing what Ruthie had said about trying to proposition her boyfriend the night before, Robert didn't have to wonder why she'd so conveniently had the condoms. A sudden suspicion made him ask, "Wait a minute. So, when you were having this dream, who exactly were you dreaming about? This jerk you've been seeing?"

She looked startled and shook her head vehemently. "No. I knew it was you."

The admission made him feel slightly better. "Thank heaven for small favors," he muttered.

"You have to understand," she said as she crossed the room to sit on the edge of the chair, "this is something I have *never* done before. Never even considered before!"

Seeing the tears fall down her cheeks, Robert tossed his jacket on the bed. Kneeling next to her, he took her hands in his own, gently stroking them until she unclenched her white fingers. "Ruthie, you can't do this to yourself. So we started out backward. We didn't go on a few boring dates before we finally had our first kiss. We didn't have to share all the details of our past relationships before we went to bed. Do you know how amazing it is for two people so perfectly in sync to find each other—and to recognize immediately how good things could be between them? How refreshing it is to experience such joy with someone else, such an immediate sense of *rightness?*"

She shot him a look of pure exasperation. "Maybe. But it mighta been kinda nice to know the *name* of the first guy who ever made me have a multiple orgasm."

Robert knew she regretted the words as soon as they left her mouth, because she dropped her face into her hands. He was unable to restrain a grin. "First, huh? Ruthie, where *have* you been digging up these men you've dated?"

Her reply was muffled in her hands.

"What?"

"I said," she replied as she lifted her eyes to meet his, "I don't want to talk about this anymore. I want to forget it ever happened."

Forget about the most erotic night of his life? Forget about a woman who would live in his dreams forever? Impossible. Robert instinctively knew that no matter what her choice now, he would wake up many mornings in the future and mentally see her beautiful sleeping face on the pillow next to his. And the sound of her laughter was something that would *always* echo in his ears.

Leaning forward, he slid his arm across her shoulder, then pressed a soft kiss on her temple. She shivered. "Do you really want to forget?" he asked, moving his mouth to her ear. He heard her sigh as he gently licked her earlobe. "Because I know I never will, Ruthie. Never."

She moaned, softly, from somewhere deep inside. Robert followed the sound, trailing his lips and tongue down her neck to press a hot kiss in the hollow of her throat. Her head fell back and Robert saw her body's reaction through the thin cotton nightshirt. Leaning lower, he pressed a hot kiss on the taut tip of her breast, breathing through the fabric, knowing the sensation was making her squirm in her seat.

"Don't tell me you're going to let this end before we ever really get started. All I've thought about since I woke up this morning is making love to you in the light of day, seeing your eyes light up when I'm inside you. Please don't tell me I'm never going to get to see that, Ruthie."

Ruthie heard him, was amazed by the sweetness of his words, but couldn't really focus on them when they were spoken right against that particular part of her anatomy. He opened his mouth, gently using his teeth to scrape the cloth against her aching nipple until she wanted to rip her own clothes right off her body.

He tried to help her. When he slid his hand under the bottom hem of her nightshirt to stroke her bare hip, Ruthie realized she had to bring herself back to reality. She bit her own lip, hard, using the sharp pain to banish the hazy, sensual cloud in which he'd effectively wrapped her.

"No," she said as she slipped out of the chair and away from him. Robert stood, reaching for her, but Ruthie held up her hands, palms out. "This is not going to happen. I'm not going to make love with a stranger."

"We're hardly strangers, sugar," he said, a tiny bit of charming southern accent creeping through his usually refined speech. "We've been properly introduced. Remember? I'm Robert, the man who gave you your first multiple orgasm."

"Thanks so much for reminding me," she said nervously. "It'd slipped my mind already!"

He took a step closer, and Ruthie backed up until the back of her legs hit the bed. "Stop it. I mean it. No sex. I have no champagne, chocolate or cold pills in my system that will allow me to forgive myself afterward!"

He stopped, obviously able to tell she was serious. "Okay, no sex. Not now."

"Okay," she said, pretending, even to herself, that

she wasn't a little disappointed. She had no idea what to say next. What did one say to an absolute stranger who'd licked her entire body like she was one sweet, giant Tootsie Pop?

"I'm hungry."

Ruthie blinked. "What?

"You said no sex. How about breakfast? I'm starved. So why don't we start getting this dating stuff out of the way by having breakfast together? If we do lunch and dinner, too, that counts as three dates, and we can meet back here tonight."

"Women typically sleep with you on the third date?"

He shrugged and offered her a self-deprecating smile. "I don't have a lot of time to date, Ruthie. Like I said last night, work is my life." His smile turned wicked. "But I think the third date is the benchmark to at least proceed to some serious foreplay."

She thought about her dreams of the night before. Correction, her *reality*. "I don't think we skimped on the foreplay," she muttered under her breath. She knew he'd heard her when he chuckled.

"So what do you say?"

Breakfast sounded innocent enough—and it counted as a date, didn't it? Even "morning after" breakfast! But there was the board meeting to consider. Not to mention that she was standing in a room in a hotel owned by her family, and members of that family were probably at this very minute working on every floor in the building. No way could she have an intimate breakfast with a stranger, in the hotel restaurant she *ran*, without someone in the Sinclair clan finding out.

"I'm sorry, Robert, but I don't think so. I need some time to think about everything that's happened."

Ruthie plucked nervously at the sleeve of her night-shirt, unable to gather the courage to look at him. "Last night changes things for me."

"Your boyfriend?"

She shook her head. "No, I don't think there was any question at the reception yesterday that we were finished."

"Then what?"

She didn't quite know how to explain it. But last night, after her humiliating episode with Bobby, she had decided to take a break from romantic entanglements and clear her head about what she needed to do next.

She was going to be thirty in a little over a year. She wanted to spend her thirties as a wife and mother, not a single working woman for whom friends set up blind dates. Now that Bobby had to be scratched off the list of potential candidates, she needed to be alone for a while to regroup, to figure out exactly how to achieve her goals.

Having a hot, purely sexual affair with an out-of-town stranger was not going to help her on her quest.

"I'm not a reckless person, believe it or not," she finally said. "I'm conservative, a homebody who'd rather stay in and play Monopoly than go out to a bar."

"I like Monopoly," he grinned, "as long as I'm the banker. Or Risk! I love that whole world domination thing."

"Why am I not surprised?"

Robert sat in a chair near the bed, crossing one ankle over the other knee, and leaning back to make himself comfortable. "So you like to play board games. I have to say that's refreshing. A lot of women I know like to play games, but not the Milton-Bradley variety."

"You know a lot of women?" she asked softly, nibbling on the tip of her index finger. She shouldn't have asked. It was none of her business. But she wanted to know.

"Know a lot, yes. See a lot, no," he replied without hesitation. "Like I said, I work long hours. I travel a great deal. And when I am home, I like to be alone."

Ruthie sighed. "I don't. It's not that I dislike my own company, but frankly, having grown up with two very busy parents, I often wished I'd had some siblings around. I'm tired of being by myself."

Feeling surprisingly unselfconscious even though she was wearing a sleepshirt in front of a man who was, for all intents and purposes, a stranger to her, she plopped on the bed. "I used to turn the radio on at night as I was drifting off to sleep, so I could pretend I had a sister sharing the room whispering with me. I was terribly jealous of my cousins and I used to tell everyone that I was Celeste's older sister and Denise was our wicked adopted stepsister."

He grinned. "Denise. The diamond flasher?"

Ruthie nodded. "Heck, there were even times I wouldn't have minded *her* being my sister! And that's saying a lot."

Robert shrugged. "Lemme tell you, siblings are *not* what they're cracked up to be. With five younger brothers to look after, I felt like I was coaching a future NBA starting lineup."

Ruthie saw an indulgent smile cross his face and knew that while he might complain about them, he was close to his family. "Sounds heavenly."

He snorted. "No. As the oldest, *I* was held responsible for everything *they* did. Never a night's sleep without a pillow fight, never a game of football without having to take one of 'em home when he got hurt. Never a date at the house without someone bringing up the subject of bodily functions."

Ruthie giggled as he winced. "But you love them."

He looked surprised she'd even asked. "Of course. They're family."

She nodded, understanding that concept. It was a given, whether you liked your relatives or not, you always loved them.

"That doesn't mean, however, that I'm not happy living hundreds of miles away from them. Especially now that three of them are married and have all these kids running around!"

"Another NBA starting lineup?"

He grinned and shook his head. "All my married brothers have girls. I do get a kick out of seeing my brother Jerry, the guy who was called "the Bulldozer" when he played for our high-school football team, dressing his two-year-old's Barbie dolls."

She smiled gently and looked away. "Yeah, my dad could sometimes get real creative with my dolls."

"You were close?"

She nodded. "I love my mom to pieces, but it was my father who was the center of my world when I was little."

"I'm sorry you lost him, Ruthie."

She tugged at her nightshirt, wanting to change the subject. "Anyway, I'm sure your brothers are real suckers for their daughters." Robert nodded, a thoughtful look on his face, leading Ruthie to wonder if he was as serious about his anti-kids stance as he'd said. "Does any of that appeal to you?"

He didn't hesitate. "Nope."

"So," she said slowly, thinking about what he'd said.

"You have no time for dating, no interest in relationships or family and you like being alone. Why do you want to see me again?"

His eyes narrowed and a wolfish grin crossed his lips. Ruthie shivered, feeling the heat from across the room. "Other than that!"

His smile softened and a look of tenderness replaced it.

"Maybe because you're the first person I've ever known who I trusted in an instant? Because I have had a smile on my face since the minute we met?"

The teasing tone disappeared, and he leaned forward in his chair, resting his elbows on his legs as he tried to convince her. "Okay, so we have different visions of our futures. But, damn, Ruthie, something serious is happening between us. I know I'll regret it for the rest of my life if I don't get a chance to explore this emotional roller coaster I've been riding with you since last night."

Ruthie's breath froze in her throat. She didn't doubt his words. He felt more for her than desire. She felt the same way. Even though it seemed impossible—since they'd known each other for less than a day—there were strong undercurrents flowing between them. They weren't merely sexual. And they scared her to death.

Trying to lighten the moment, Ruthie chuckled. "Yeah, well, believe it or not, there are one or two things that have happened to me since we met that I'd have to say were firsts."

Robert stood and walked across the room. Ruthie watched him, noting again the grace of his movements. In the light of day and fully clothed he was just as devastatingly attractive as he'd been the night before. If he tried to sit down on the bed and take her into his arms, she didn't know if she'd be able to resist. She didn't know if she really wanted to.

"I'm not going to pressure you. You said you had a meeting this morning, so I'll leave you alone for a while," he said. "Think about it. Give us a shot."

Ruthie was grateful he'd remembered her meeting— if left up to her, she might have forgotten about it entirely! "That's probably for the best. I do have a lot to think about and I need to be alone to clear my head," Ruthie said.

Robert nodded and retrieved his jacket from the bed. "All right. We'll retreat to our separate corners for a while. But will you at least consider meeting me back in the hotel kitchen tonight at midnight for some of that cheesecake?" He moved closer, leaning over her, and slid his fingers into her mussed hair, pushing a few strands behind her ears. "We'll just talk and laugh some more and get to know each other better."

The temptation to take him up on his offer was sharp and intense. It went completely against everything she'd told herself about how foolish it would be to get any further involved with him, but that didn't seem to matter right now. "You're staying on at the hotel?"

"For several days at least," he said with a grin, obviously realizing she was considering it. "Come on, Ruthie, say yes."

Ruthie took a deep breath and closed her eyes. She was checking out of her suite and going home to her own apartment today, but she lived only a few miles away. Slipping back into the kitchen would be absolutely no problem. And, if she really was going to organize her love life, set her sights on one man and get herself married before the age of thirty, maybe one fi-

nal reckless fling with someone totally unsuitable—
and totally devastating—wouldn't be such a bad idea.

Finally, with less reluctance than she would ever
have admitted, she nodded her head. "Midnight."

5

AFTER RUTHIE WAS showered, dressed, and as in control of her wildly swinging emotions as possible, she gathered her belongings and left her room. She stashed her overnight bag—complete with the rolled-up bridesmaid dress from hell—in her car, wishing she could get in and drive home. Impossible, of course, because of the board meeting. Her uncle Henry had flat-out ordered every family member to be in attendance. That included her great-aunts Lila and Flossie, neither of whom could stand to miss their weekday morning episodes of *The Price Is Right*. It *had* to be serious if they were going to tear themselves away from Bob Barker, whom Aunt Flossie described as a "hottie."

Making her way to the front desk, she cast a critical eye around the lobby, noting the worn patches on the burgundy brocade sofas. Her father would never have allowed them to remain in such condition, but Ruthie couldn't fault her uncle Henry too much. Heaven knew the man tried. Whereas Ruthie's father had been born with a talent for managing the Kerrigan, his younger twin brother wasn't so blessed.

Approaching the check-in desk, Ruthie smiled at her aunt Elise—mother of Celeste, Denise and Chuck—who was also the daytime front desk manager. Though only a Sinclair by marriage to Ruthie's uncle Henry,

Elise loved the Kerrigan as much as any full-blooded member of the family.

That was saying a lot, considering the hotel had been in the Sinclair family since the 1930s. Ruthie's great-grandfather had picked up the building for a song after its former owner, one Evander L. Pickering, had taken a leap off the top floor back in 1929, earning the hotel the nickname "Pickering's Dive."

Renamed the Kerrigan Towers, the hotel reached its heyday in the 1960s, when Ruthie's father had taken charge. But when he'd passed away, nearly twelve years ago, his brother, her uncle Henry, had taken over. Things had steadily declined ever since.

Everyone in the family knew it. And everyone had feared the day someone else would recognize the Kerrigan's financial position and make a move on the hotel. But they didn't worry too much. First of all, the hotel was small, only six stories tall with less than a hundred rooms. It was not in business to compete with the luxurious national chains that dotted Chestnut Street in downtown Philadelphia. Instead, the Kerrigan catered to the leisure traveler who wanted the right address for less money than a Hyatt or a Marriott would charge. They weren't going to be gobbled up by a competitor, because they didn't have enough to entice one. Nor would a low-end chain want the hassle and expense of updating the antique building to conform with franchise requirements.

Plus, the hotel stock was all closely held by family members. No one could forcibly take control of the Kerrigan if the Sinclairs remained united. And one thing that could be said for Ruthie's family—when they had a common enemy, they were a formidable force.

"Good morning, dear, did you sleep well? You look a little peaked," her aunt said in her pleasant "have a nice day" voice.

Though she looked utterly harmless, with her sweet, unlined face and neatly pulled back graying blond hair, Ruthie's aunt Elise was the Olympic champion at sniffing out lies. Ruthie pretended she hadn't heard. "All ready to check out," she said brightly. "I don't suppose you've seen the bride and groom up and about yet this morning, have you?"

As expected, the older woman was immediately distracted. "Oh, of course not, and your uncle Henry should be ashamed of himself for making those children stay here when they should have left for their honeymoon last night. Wasn't my Celeste a beautiful bride though?"

"She was," Ruthie replied with complete sincerity.

"Now you're the last single Sinclair woman, dear. Got any prospects?"

Ruthie just shrugged.

"That young man you've been dating was looking a little green around the gills last night. Then he hurried away before the cake was even cut. Not very mannerly, you know."

"We're finished, Aunt Elise."

Her aunt's obvious disapproval of Bobby's bad manners wasn't enough to hide her disappointment that another marital prospect had slipped off Ruthie's hook. She sighed. "Maybe things aren't so bad and he'll come around!"

Yeah, sure, he'll come around, especially when he finds out I had hot amazing sex with a stranger three times last night!

"I don't want him to come around, Elise. He wasn't

right for me. I want the kind of man who will get down on the floor and crawl after our babies."

Her aunt paled, her small hands flying up off the desk like fluttering birds. "Babies? Oh, saints preserve us, Ruthie, you're not..."

"No! I'm not pregnant." Ruthie tempered her vehemence with a shaky chuckle. "I'm speaking figuratively. I want a family man who wants loads of kids and a quiet, stay-at-home lifestyle. Not an uptight accountant type like Bobby."

Ruthie had a quick image of Robert Kendall, who'd admitted to being a workaholic, and wondered why in heck she'd agreed to meet him that night. He was so obviously the opposite of the kind of man she needed, in spite of how physically attracted she was to him.

But, when she thought about it, she had to admit that it was more than raw physical attraction. She'd really, truly liked him from the moment they met. She'd been drawn to him, both emotionally and physically, before he'd ever touched her. Ruthie had felt that instant connection he'd talked about, and she had sensed, as he had, that something pretty amazing could happen between them.

So she was going to be brave, daring, and explore the possibilities, instead of living to regret the wasted opportunity.

Besides, the things that man could do with his mouth...

Ruthie gave her head a shake and looked at her aunt. "Well, uh, I'm going to check things in the kitchen. Let me know if you see Celeste, I'd like to speak to her before the board meeting to see how she liked her little surprise this morning."

"Surprise?"

"I had an elaborate breakfast delivered to their room."

"Wonderful! Still, it's a shame they're not having that breakfast at a hotel in the Caribbean."

"Celeste wanted to be in on whatever's happening at the board meeting this morning. Though I'm sure it's nothing major." Ruthie saw her aunt immediately busy her hands shuffling blank registration forms. "Aunt Elise? You don't think something serious is going on, do you?"

Her aunt wouldn't meet her eye, and Ruthie felt her first real sense of misgiving over this morning's meeting. Her uncle had been so adamant that all family members—including Celeste, the bride—must attend, which hadn't made much sense to anyone. After all, every bit of Kerrigan's stock was held by members of the Sinclair family. Even if they were indeed being eyed for a takeover no company would be able to force them to sell if the family didn't all agree. That was their one safety net, the one thing Ruthie and the younger generation of Sinclairs counted on—that the Kerrigan would be in Sinclair hands until one of them stepped up to take over as manager. Ruthie, Denise, Celeste and Chuck had even talked about it on occasion. And it was with perfect agreement that they'd all realized Celeste would be the one for the job once her father stepped down. "What do you know, Elise?"

"Well...I don't know *all* the details."

Ruthie gritted her teeth. "Tell me."

Elise darted a quick look around, making sure no one could overhear. "Did you read the memo about the hotel's mortgage being sold several months ago?"

Ruthie's confusion must have shown on her face because Elise frowned. "I didn't think so. I don't think anyone did, which is exactly what Henry was hoping when he buried that little detail in the middle of a long, boring financial memo! I would never have known myself if I hadn't overheard him talking to someone from the accounting firm the other day."

"So the mortgage was sold."

Elise nodded, and waggled her eyebrows knowingly, as if she'd told Ruthie a state secret. Trying not to smile, Ruthie asked, "What does that have to do with today's board meeting?"

"Well," Elise continued, leaning forward to whisper, "what if the new mortgage holder isn't quite as understanding of the slow nature of payment to which the Kerrigan is accustomed? And what if some other group out there is trying to use that fact to gain financial control over the hotel? That's the gist of what I overheard. The mortgage is overdue and we're being targeted by some hotel chain."

The older woman crossed her arms, the worry on her face not quite hiding her satisfaction at having revealed a secret.

"Impossible," Ruthie declared. "Who in their right mind would go to that much trouble to take over one old, elegant but falling-apart hotel?"

Elise sniffed, obviously offended that Ruthie didn't believe her. "I hope you're right. I just hope you are."

Ruthie shook her head slowly. "I'm sure I am, Elise. Maybe we just need to meet to talk about restructuring our debt. That reroofing project went over budget last year. I'm sure it's something like that. There's no way we could be in serious trouble. I'm certain of it."

LATER THAT MORNING, Ruthie made her way to the boardroom for the meeting. The offices were located in the old basement of the hotel, almost directly beneath the kitchen, and Ruthie passed through the restaurant, intent on taking the back stairs.

She should have known better. There was no way she could get past the wait staff, or the Monday chef, without being waylaid with a myriad of problems. She put out as many figurative fires as she could, clenching her teeth to avoid arguing with Francois, the French pastry chef who came in on Mondays and Wednesdays to prepare special desserts for the restaurant.

Francois was a pain in the rear, as far as Ruthie was concerned. Her uncle Henry, however, loved that they could tout authentic French pastries. Though Ruthie was perfectly capable of producing exactly the same desserts, especially after the year she'd spent at a culinary school in Paris, her uncle liked the cachet that came with Francois's foreign-sounding name. So Ruthie had to let him in her kitchen. There had been times Ruthie was tempted to get her old English-to-French dictionary and throw some real French phrases in the man's direction, to see if he knew what the heck she was talking about. Francois's accent sometimes seemed a little thin, and she had to wonder if he had embellished his background. For all she knew, he could really be some guy named Frankie from Hoboken.

This morning Francois was on a tirade. Finally after his ten-minute tantrum, Ruthie was able to discern his complaint. He was having trouble keeping his cream in his éclairs.

"I don't have time to hear about your personal problems," Ruthie muttered under her breath when she could finally get a word in. The chef didn't hear her, but the guy washing dishes did. Ruthie saw his shoulders shake with laughter.

Glancing at the clock, she realized she was going to be late. Ruthie promised to come back later, pushed past the ranting chef, and raced for the stairs.

ROBERT WAS FEELING very pleased with himself and quite confident as the board meeting with the Sinclair family started. Based on the Kerrigan Towers's financial situation, he hadn't figured taking over the hotel would pose much of a challenge. Poor management was obviously behind the hotel's financial situation, and poor management was usually quick to unload their problems if the price was right. It would be. Winchester Inns was a big company, but they weren't bullies. Robert played fair; the compensation the Sinclair family would receive was more than generous.

That was probably a good thing, because, with this group, he didn't know if they'd even be able to look out for themselves. The board was unprofessional, and, to put it frankly, just a little bit strange.

The two old ladies were a prime example. A study in opposites, they were apparently the daughters of the Sinclair who'd first bought the Kerrigan. That would put them somewhere in their eighties, but they sure didn't act like it. Robert would swear the large one sitting nearest the door, Lila, had been flirting with him, fluttering her eyelashes and once even dropping a wink, right up until the reason for the meeting was announced. Then she'd glared daggers in his direction and thrust her imposing chest at him. Feeling like he was looking down the barrels of two cannons, he'd had to glance away.

The other old one, introduced as Flossie, wore a tight dress decorated with florid purple flowers. A ridiculous matching plumed hat was perched atop her blue-gray hair. She was tiny, not nearly as imposing as the first. Flossie's sweet smile and gentle blue eyes were deceptive, though. Because in the few minutes before the meeting had started, Robert had observed the woman stealing not one, not two, but three different items from the table. She'd first snatched a gold pen right off the pad of paper in front of Henry Sinclair, her nephew, who sat next to her. She grinned as she tucked it into her suitcase-sized purse. Then she'd gone a step further and taken his entire notebook. The coup de grace came when she tossed the contents of her water glass over her right shoulder, hitting the potted palm behind her, then shook the last few drops onto the back of Henry's black suit. Zip, into the bag it went.

No, Robert couldn't say he was much concerned about a fight from the oldest generation of the Sinclair family.

The next group was comprised of Henry Sinclair, current manager of the hotel, and his wife, Elise. Henry looked quiet, unassuming, not at all forceful enough to manage a first-class establishment in today's competitive travel industry.

The youngest generation didn't appear to offer much of a challenge, either. Henry and Elise Sinclair had three adult children. The boy, well, young man, wore a shaggy blond haircut and lazy grin that told Robert he would probably be very interested in being financially able to quit working inside and hit the beach. The other two were women, and one he instantly pegged as very money conscious. The look on her face as she'd sized up Monica, and Monica's wardrobe, had been a dead giveaway. But her sister, the tall blonde, had given him a moment's worry. She looked sharp, met his eye directly, shook his hand without flinching. So far this one, young though she was, appeared to be the only one on the board he might have problems with.

Until Ruthie walked through the door.

WHEN RUTHIE HAD reached the conference room doors and seen them closed tightly, she'd paused to slow her breathing and smooth her mussed hair. Pasting on a calm, collected look, she'd walked into the meeting, feeling terribly self-conscious at strolling in ten minutes past the hour.

Now every set of eyes turned in her direction. Disappointment shone through her uncle Henry's frown. "Ruthie, you're late."

"I'm so sorry, I got sidetracked upstairs," she explained as she took a seat closest to the door, avoiding looking around the table at her relatives.

"All right, now perhaps we can get on with the meeting," the older man said, with a dignified nod of his head. The nod caused the one long strand of graying blond hair—which Uncle Henry generally kept combed from the right side of his head all the way over to the left in a vain attempt to hide a bald spot—to fall forward until it nearly brushed his eyebrows. Ruthie bit her lip to prevent a chuckle from slipping out. But when she caught Celeste's eye, across the table, she noticed the strained expression on her cousin's face. Celeste wasn't laughing. Something was really wrong.

"As I was explaining to the board, we are gathered here to listen to a proposal from Winchester Hotels. Their representatives are here to tell us about their—" Uncle Henry coughed once into his fist "—*offer* to take over the Kerrigan Towers."

Ruthie sucked in a deep breath, unable to believe

Elise had been right. Jerking her attention to the far end of the huge conference table, she noticed two people sitting there.

The woman was striking, a slim brunette wearing a bored expression on her perfectly made-up face. Next to her, sitting almost sideways so Ruthie couldn't get a good look at him, was a dark-haired man. He held his hand beside his cheek, and sat slumped down in his chair, nearly blocked from her view by the people between them at the table. Ruthie leaned back, trying to look past her great-aunt Lila, whose girth made her hard to see around. Lila fortunately cooperated, choosing that moment to lean forward and rest her intimidating chest on the heavy oak table. Ruthie figured if she'd listened for it, she would have heard the antique wood groan in protest.

Lila's new position, and the shifting of chairs on down the table, gave Ruthie a clean line of sight to the other side of the room, and she took advantage of it.

She wished she hadn't. As her breath left her body in one long, smooth whoosh, she found herself staring directly into a set of features she'd memorized the night before. His huge, brown eyes looked guilty as sin.

"Son of a..." she mumbled slowly.

It was Robert. Robert, the man with whom she'd spent the previous night in dreamy passion. The man who'd gently kissed her on the lips when she'd agreed to meet him in the kitchen later. All the while knowing what he was going to do!

"I can't believe this."

Robert closed his eyes, hoping they were playing tricks on him. Maybe some other curvy little redhead had just entered the boardroom. When he looked again, his hopes were dashed. It was Ruthie. And the expression on her face was pretty indicative of her mood. She looked like she wanted to kill him. Not just kill, but maim and torture, too. Slowly. With rusty tools.

"Ruthie, is something wrong?" her uncle asked. Robert saw her look around at the others in the room, realizing they were all staring at her. Her face grew pink and her jaw clenched. Then her eyes met his again and one message shone through loud and clear: *This is not over.*

"Mr. Kendall? I believe you may proceed," Henry Sinclair said after Ruthie crossed her arms in front of her chest and sat back heavily in her chair.

Feeling as though an invisible hand was pressing down upon his shoulders, Robert took a deep breath then slowly stood up. "You all have in front of you a prospectus detailing the hotel's financial situation." He saw Ruthie's glance dart around quickly, then she snatched up a sheaf of papers and began flipping through them. "As you can see, the Kerrigan is several months in arrears on its mortgage. Winchester Hotels is interested in buying the Kerrigan, removing your debt and leaving you all with a tidy profit."

"Or what?" Ruthie snarled as she tossed the papers back onto the table. They slid across the smooth oak surface directly toward the old lady, Flossie. Robert watched the woman scoop them up and shove them into her bottomless satchel. No one else seemed to notice.

"I'm not sure what you're asking, Miss...*Sinclair*? Ruth Sinclair?" Robert asked, hearing the accusation in his own voice. Why hadn't she told him her last name? Why the hell hadn't he *asked*?

"Right. Mr. Kendall of *Winchester Hotels*. My name is

Ruth Sinclair, I'm a member of the family, a member of the board, and head chef of this hotel."

"Chef?" Robert gritted his teeth as he remembered finding her in the kitchen the night before. No wonder she'd felt free to help herself to dessert! "I didn't realize that."

"How could you?" she snapped. "We obviously don't know a single thing about each other!"

Robert saw some of the other board members looking on with interest, though they said nothing. "I suppose we don't," he murmured. "But that doesn't mean we have to be enemies. We can work together...."

"Save it. Just save the speeches. Obviously you know what you're doing in the *board*room and have lots of tricks up your sleeve to help you get what you want. Namely the Kerrigan. So let's cut through all the other garbage. I want to know the bottom line. If we say no, thank you, we don't want to sell, what will you do then? Will you and your *business associate* quietly go back to wherever you came from?"

Catching the pointed glance Ruthie cast toward Monica, Robert winced. Ruthie had put things together quickly. She obviously remembered his claim that he was using the room key to go visit his business associate in the middle of the night. Judging by the fire in her green eyes, and the way her full lips were pulled tightly over her clenched teeth, he could tell Ruthie was thinking exactly what he'd feared she would.

Before he could reply, Monica interrupted. "You don't have any choice. The mortgage company you're dealing with happens to be a subsidiary of Winchester Enterprises. We own the note. If you don't sell, we can simply call the loan. You'll never come up with the money and no one else is going to refinance with your credit and debt. Then we'll just take the hotel."

Chaos erupted in the room and Robert felt like strangling Monica. But it was *his* fault she'd blown the meeting. From the minute they'd first met in the lobby this morning, she'd been furious that he'd stood her up the night before. She'd been waiting for a chance to let off steam, and, unfortunately, here in the boardroom was where she'd chosen to erupt.

"Please, ladies and gentlemen, don't get the wrong idea. Winchester Hotels does not want to steal the Kerrigan from you." He cast a pleading glance in Ruthie's direction, mentally willing her to trust him, to give him a chance to explain. "We are here to make you a legitimate, generous offer, which we hope you'll seriously consider. There are no hidden agendas, you don't need to fear anything underhanded. I'm going to be completely honest and open with you."

She made a rude sound of disbelief, muttering, "Yeah, right. Let's crown the King of Honesty."

Robert knew if Ruthie were really able to "crown" him at that moment it would be with a two-ton boulder.

"We need to listen to what they have to say," Henry Sinclair said, looking as if it pained him to utter the words. "Please, let's look this over and hear them out."

Though there was much huffing and mumbling, the board members turned their attention back to the folders before them. Before Robert could say another word, he saw Ruthie lean across the conference table. "Aunt Flossie...my papers, please?"

The sweet-looking old lady woman feigned a look of complete surprise and innocence, her blue eyes as guileless as a child's. Then, when Ruthie frowned and mouthed something at her, the old woman muttered, "Oh, all right," dug into her bag for the prospectus and slid it back across the table. The exchange took less than thirty seconds and no one else in the room paid a bit of attention.

After that, the meeting progressed as smoothly as could be expected. Even under normal circumstances Robert never looked forward to these kinds of situations, when board members had to make tough choices. In this case, considering a woman with whom he'd been lying naked hours before was glaring at him like he'd just intentionally run over her dog, it was much worse. When she finally turned her attention toward Monica, a speculative expression crossed her face. Then she wouldn't look at him at all, which was just as well since he didn't imagine he would have liked the disdain he felt sure he'd see in her eyes.

He couldn't believe the bad luck. Robert had never considered himself an exceptionally lucky person. He'd always relied on his own abilities to get what he'd wanted. But since the night before, he'd been feeling like a guy walking around with a winning lottery ticket in his pocket. Ever since he'd met *her*, Ruthie Sinclair, he'd for some reason felt like he could take over the world.

Unfortunately, what he was out to take over was her beloved family's livelihood.

If they hadn't been opponents in this financial game of chicken over the hotel, Robert would have admired the hell out of the way she handled herself. It was obvious that Ruthie and her blond cousin, Celeste, were the two strongest-willed people in the room. Other than himself, of course.

She asked intuitive questions, put aside her own animosity toward him to go through the Winchester proposal point by point. And she and Celeste managed to concisely tear it apart. She zeroed in on problems he hadn't even considered. What she missed, Celeste caught. Henry Sinclair, Ruthie's uncle, didn't say much, and the rest of the board stayed out of the discussion completely.

He had to admit he was impressed by her. If they hadn't been adversaries, he'd have felt like applauding when she was finished. Then he thought about it. Adversaries? Lovers? Both? Neither? All Robert knew was that within less than twenty-four hours his orderly world had turned upside down, inside out and bassackward. And all because of the cute little redhead who was turning him on even as she glared daggers at him.

RUTHIE USED every bit of restraint she had to maintain her composure throughout the meeting. She wanted to scream. She wanted to throw something. She wanted to pick up one of the potted plants and dump a bunch of dirt all over Robert Kendall's gorgeous lying head.

Instead, she chewed on the inside of her cheek, clenched the fabric of her skirt in her fists, and listened calmly while he outlined a plan to ruin her life. Then she'd gone over that plan and done whatever she could to poke huge gaping holes through it.

As the meeting went on, one thought repeated in her brain with the regularity of a ticking clock: They couldn't lose the Kerrigan.

The Sinclair family simply could not let this beautiful, grand old building fall into the clutches of a slick company that would remove every bit of character the place had. They'd turn it into a clone of every other Winchester in the world.

She glanced around the table, gauging the family's reaction to what was happening. Henry and Elise simply looked stricken. Though Aunt Lila remained rigid and skeptical, Ruthie had seen the interest in the old woman's eyes when the financial figures started getting tossed around. It had been matched by Denise's, and even, to some extent, Chuck's. Celeste remained resolute, fortunately. And Aunt Flossie ignored everything around her, happily digging through her goodies in her bag.

So, Aunt Lila, Denise, and perhaps Chuck might be swayed. The rest wouldn't. The other family members who held stock in the hotel—distant cousins, even Ruthie's own honeymooning mother—didn't have enough to make much difference one way or another. If they could convince the Sinclairs in this room to remain united, they had a good chance at beating this thing.

It wasn't merely her affection for the building that made her so determined to fight. Nearly every memory Ruthie had of her childhood somehow involved the Kerrigan Towers. In the twelve years since her father's death, Ruthie had used the hotel to help visualize him, picturing him sitting behind the desk in his office, or walking sedately through the lobby to greet their guests. He'd been more than a manager, he'd been a host, giving their wealthy clientele the gracious friendliness one would expect of a family member. He'd had Henry's gentle smile, but had backed it up with keen intelligence and an innate understanding of how to make their visitors happy.

Ruthie's earliest birthday parties had been in the hotel game room, she'd taken her first steps, so she was told, just a few feet away from the outdoor swimming pool. Her father had scooped her up before she could fall in!

She'd spent her summers lurking in the kitchens, first snitching treats from the chef and later watching him work, wanting to know how he created the marvelous delicacies they served. As a teenager, she'd waited tables in the restaurant, pitched in to clean when the housekeeping department was short-staffed. She'd worked the front desk, fixed vending machines, run extra towels up to guests and even carried luggage a time or two. Coming back to the hotel after going to college and culinary school had been a foregone conclusion.

And this man, this beautiful, dark-eyed stranger who'd made her feel things she'd never felt before in her life, wanted to take that from her? To take not only her job, but her family's history, her childhood memories, and the last tangible connection she felt with the father she'd lost as a teenager?

"No way," she mumbled softly. There was no way in hell she was going to let it happen.

6

SHE WASN'T GOING to show up. Robert had known it before he'd stealthily made his way into the hotel kitchen just before midnight. And now, at half past the hour, he admitted it to himself. Ruthie wasn't going to meet him at their spot.

Their spot? Right. Twenty-four hours into a relationship and he was thinking in terms of "their spot."

"Get over yourself," he muttered in disgust as he tried to open one of the large refrigerators. The door wouldn't budge. "Bet she locked it on purpose."

He'd been crazy to come down here, nuts to think she'd actually keep their midnight date. Considering what had happened after the board meeting, he wondered why he'd wanted her to.

That morning, during the meeting, Ruthie's fury had mounted throughout Robert's presentation to the board. Whenever she wasn't bringing up every negative point she could think of, he'd seen her lips moving as she muttered to herself and had known she was mentally telling him off.

He'd wanted to get her alone as soon as the meeting was over and try, somehow, to straighten things out. Unfortunately, after his presentation, he'd been ushered out and the family had remained in a closed-door session. He'd hung around near the elevator for over an hour waiting for it to end.

Monica hadn't bothered waiting with him. She was still giving him the silent treatment as payment for not showing up the night before. Not for the first time in his life, he'd wondered what on earth made women think that was an effective way to deal with men. He'd seen his mother do it to his father, his sisters-in-law do it to his brothers, and he'd never understood it. With Monica ignoring him, he felt much more grateful than punished!

When the meeting had finally let up, Ruthie had been one of the last to leave the boardroom. She and her young cousin, Celeste, had remained inside with one or two others. Robert had withstood the curious looks from other family members as they passed him in the hall. For the most part they'd ignored him, although he'd swear the large elderly one intentionally bumped into him, nearly knocking him down with her fearsome bosom. If it'd been the petite one, he'd have immediately checked his pocket to be sure she hadn't lifted his wallet.

When Ruthie finally emerged, he began to understand the effectiveness of the silent treatment. She sailed right past him, her little nose stuck up in the air, not sparing him so much as a glance as she disappeared behind a door marked Private.

It was only later in the afternoon, when he'd ducked into an elevator right before the doors closed, that he'd been able to catch her alone. She still hadn't spoken. He'd spilled his guts, begging her to listen to him, telling her how sorry he was for being the one to bring this bad news to her family.

She hadn't said a word. She'd simply waited until the elevator doors opened with a soft swish, then used the deadly, sharp high heel of her shoe to try to stomp a hole in his foot before stepping out.

The fact that she'd nearly crippled him hadn't stopped Robert from immediately going after her. Unfortunately, he'd found his way suddenly blocked by a bellhop with a heavily loaded luggage cart. By the time Robert had limped around the cart, Ruthie had disappeared. Not seeing her again for the rest of the day, he'd assumed she'd left to return to her apartment, which she'd said was close by.

Thinking she'd show up in the kitchen tonight had been delusional. She was going to do everything in her power to avoid him, obviously blaming him for what was going wrong with her family business. As if *he* was the one who'd made unsound financial decisions for the past decade and put the hotel in jeopardy!

"Damn, she could've broken my foot," he muttered aloud, as he stood indecisively in the darkened hotel kitchen. Robert thrust his hands through his hair. "She's crazy. And I'm crazier for wanting to see her again!"

But he did. He wanted to see her again. Badly. He wanted to talk to her, to listen to her laugh. To get caught up in her giggle and feel his world tilt on its axis with a flash of those dimples in her cheeks.

He wanted to make love to her, in the bright, broad daylight. Wanted to see her lovely green eyes watching every touch, fully aware of every caress, with no darkened room, no champagne, no cold medication to interfere with her honest responses.

He leaned against the butcher-block table, closing his eyes to savor the memories of the night before. It had been astounding, overwhelming, the best sexual experience of his life. And it went beyond physical, for some crazy reason. Their passion and tenderness had triggered an emotional response in him that was completely unexpected given that they were practically strangers.

Robert Kendall did not believe in love at first sight. That notion was beyond his realm of imagination. But this…this connection he felt to Ruthie Sinclair was more than attraction, more than intrigue. He didn't know how to put it into words.

He did know that it was unlike anything he'd ever experienced. For the first time in nearly a decade he was more interested in another person than he was in his job. And for the first time *ever*, he actually envisioned bringing a woman home to North Carolina, knowing Ruthie could hold her own among the Kendall clan.

"But why the hell would you want to do that?" he asked himself. Why was he even thinking in those terms? He and Ruthie were opposites. She obviously liked being tied to this old building, with her family roots sunk firmly into its concrete foundation. Robert's foundation was far from concrete. It was flexible, mobile—he had a foothold in North Carolina, another in New York, while the rest of the world beckoned him to explore it.

Even if they could resolve all their other differences—the hotel, their discordant personalities, desires for the future and views of the world—there was still the small fact that they lived hundreds of miles apart.

Telling himself it was better ended, that getting any more involved with Ruthie Sinclair was going to seriously mess with his head and screw up his plans for the Kerrigan Towers, he stalked toward the exit. But, just as he was about to push through the swinging

doors, a note above a wall phone caught his attention.
"In case of emergency, contact..." Right below it was
the name Ruthie Sinclair. Her phone number.

And her address.

THE TICKING OF THE plastic black-cat clock on her bedroom wall was slowly driving Ruthie right out of her
mind. She lay in the darkness, seeking sleep the way
someone in the desert would seek water, but it
wouldn't come. If it wasn't the click-click of the cat's
long tail, swinging in time to each second, it was the
humming of the air-conditioning flipping on, or the
rumble of a passing car in the parking lot. Or just her
own thoughts shooting around in her brain, bouncing
off the interior of her skull, unwilling to be silent.

Heaven knew she should be asleep already. She certainly hadn't gotten much rest the night before, from
what she could remember. "Don't think about *that*,
Ruthie Sinclair!" she told herself.

No, she couldn't think about last night. Couldn't remember his hands on her skin or the roughness of his
cheek as he traced a path down the side of her neck
with his tongue. His lips, his body, the physical feeling
of him inside her, the sensation that lingered even now,
leaving her weak-limbed and languorous nearly
twenty-four hours later. The impressions of their night
together were stamped somewhere deep inside her
brain, coming out of nowhere to hit her with sudden
flashes of memory, like her best dreams often did. *But
it wasn't a dream!*

"This is impossible," she muttered as she thrust back
the covers of her bed and got up. She needed to do
something. Actually, she needed to *eat* something—but
two nights in a row of chocolate indulgence was

strictly against the yo-yo dieter's rulebook. "Fruit salad."

She didn't bother pulling a robe on over her blue cotton nightshirt. Heading into the kitchen, Ruthie raided the crisper drawer in her refrigerator and grabbed as much fresh fruit as she could find. Preparing food always distracted her. Even on her worst days, throwing together ingredients to make a delicious dish could always make her feel better.

She ignored the siren's call of the Ben & Jerry's New York Super Fudge Chunk in the freezer and got to work washing and dicing a melon, pears, grapes and berries. She'd retrieved some sliced almonds and stuck them in the toaster oven to brown when she heard a knock.

"Pretty late, boys," she muttered, glancing at the clock, which was moving past 1:00 a.m. It wasn't unusual for the two college-age single guys in the apartment next to hers to have parties with late-arriving guests on weekends. She'd even gone to one or two of them, before realizing there were a heck of a lot of years between twenty-one and twenty-eight. Being around a bunch of college kids made her feel way too old!

Usually she didn't mind the parties, but, after all, tonight was a work night. She imagined Mrs. Humphries downstairs was already preparing to whack the ceiling with a broom handle.

Remembering the kiwi she'd picked up at the produce stand the week before, she dug two out, and also snagged a banana from a basket on the counter. She was about to place them on the cutting board when the knock came again. This time she realized the noise was not coming from her neighbor's door. It was coming from her own.

Not even pausing to drop the fruit, she hurried through her small living room, wondering who on earth would be showing up this late at night.

"He wouldn't dare," she said indignantly as she peeked through the peephole and saw Robert Kendall. He was lifting his hand to knock again. Mindful of her nosy neighbors, Ruthie snatched the door open before he could do it. "What on earth do you think you're doing here?"

"You stood me up."

She didn't understand what he was talking about. "What?"

"Our date," he explained as he leaned against the doorjamb, as nonchalant and casual as if he were simply paying a Sunday afternoon visit to an old friend. "Midnight. The hotel kitchen. Remember?"

Ruthie let out a snort of laughter. "Yeah, right, like I was really going to want to meet with you again. It's bad enough I'm going to have to see you in a business setting."

"You didn't seem to mind seeing me in a social setting last night," he said with a wicked grin.

Ruthie frowned, glaring at him. "Don't. Just don't even try being all charming and cute and sexy because right now I hate your lousy guts."

"Ouch. That's pretty strong. I seem to recall, however, that about this time twenty-four hours ago you felt anything but hatred for me. Don't tell me you've forgotten already? Or is it that you don't quite remember everything from last night? I could tell you all about it. I haven't forgotten a moment."

She swallowed hard, closing her eyes as flashes of

memory assaulted her. He'd pegged it—she hadn't forgotten, but she still wasn't clear on all the details. That probably made the hollow need inside her body even worse. The impressions she had of his touch and his kiss made her ache to experience those things while fully conscious.

"Not gonna happen," she muttered, more to herself than to him as she opened her eyes. She didn't kid herself that resisting him would be easy—he looked too darn good for that. He was dressed differently tonight. No suit, no sports coat, just tight jeans and a black T-shirt that outlined his muscular chest and clung to his thick arms. If she hadn't already spent the evening hours tossing and turning in her bed, remembering bits and pieces of their lovemaking, seeing him now would have forcibly reminded her.

Ruthie clenched her jaw and fought to clear her head. All it took was the thought of the nasty surprise she'd received in the boardroom at the hotel that morning to snap her out of the sensual spell she'd fallen into since opening the door. "You're wasting your time."

Glancing at Robert, she saw his attention focused a foot or two below her face. He wore a very unusual expression, a combination of laughter and something that looked almost like pain. She followed his stare and looked down to behold the two fuzzy little kiwi fruit and the banana, which she still clutched in her left hand. Then she looked back at Robert and frowned. "Why can men find sexual connotations in absolutely everything?"

He lifted one eyebrow and tilted his head. "Come on, Ruthie, you gotta admit..."

"I'm not admitting a thing," she said as she crossed her arms, effectively hiding the fruit behind her back.

"Look, I didn't come over here to play sexy word games," he said. "I want to talk to you."

Before Ruthie could respond, a piercing whine emanated from the direction of her kitchen. Recognizing the smoke alarm, she remembered the almonds, turned her back on Robert and raced away. Dropping the fruit on the counter, she grabbed a pot holder and yanked the tray of blackened nuts out of the toaster oven, then unplugged the thing for good measure.

Though she hadn't even noticed Robert following her, she realized he had when she saw him standing on a chair outside the kitchen door, waving a dish towel in front of the smoke detector until it stopped shrieking. "That was a close one."

"It was your fault. You distracted me."

"Why were you baking something at this time of night?" he asked as he climbed down from the chair and entered the kitchen.

"That's your fault, too!" She dumped the burned nuts down the sink and ran them through the garbage disposal. "I wasn't able to sleep because my mind was too caught up thinking about what you're trying to do to me."

"Hey, I haven't even touched you for over seventeen hours," he said, holding up his hands in a defensive posture. He leaned back against the counter to watch her work.

"You know perfectly well what I'm talking about," Ruthie said as she spread a fresh batch of almonds on the small baking sheet and slid them back into the toaster oven, this time keeping the door open and watching them closely.

"I'm not trying to do anything to hurt you, Ruthie. I'm sorry I was the one who had to bring the Kerrigan's financial situation to your attention, but you can't hold me personally responsible. And it shouldn't have anything to do with *us*."

He sounded perfectly reasonable, as usual, and that made Ruthie even angrier. "Not have anything to do with us? There *is* no us! If there were an us, maybe you'd have an inkling about how devastating the idea of losing the Kerrigan is to me and my family."

He stepped closer and suddenly Ruthie realized how small her apartment kitchen was. He filled it up, blocking her view of the refrigerator with those impossibly wide shoulders. His biceps strained against the black cotton and Ruthie had a sudden image of how simple it would be for him to lift her onto the counter and step between her thighs.

"Last night was like nothing I've ever known," he said, his voice still quiet, absolutely hypnotic. "If you're honest with yourself, you'll admit you feel the same way, Ruthie. Don't let some business deal get in the way of exploring what is going on between us. And don't try to deny that something *is* going on between us!"

He stepped closer. She craned her head all the way back to look up at him, and was startled by the tenderness in his brown eyes. Tenderness? From a corporate shark out to ruin her life? No. She had to be seeing things. But his lips quirked up into a gentle smile and her heart did a funny flip-flop in her chest.

"Last night was pure magic, from the minute we met. Don't throw away our chance to find out why, Ruthie." He came closer, his eyes studying her face, lingering on her lips, which parted as her breath came harder from her lungs. "Please don't tell me I'm never going to get to touch you again, hold you, make you come apart in my arms and watch it happen, certain I've never seen anything more beautiful in my life."

That got to her. Now he was definitely hitting below the belt. Ruthie felt her legs go weak and shaky as her body reacted to his words. Just his voice, speaking in a low seductive tone, and she was wet, quivering, and ready to experience more of the pleasure she remembered from the night before. He was slipping past her defenses, climbing toward her through the invisible aura of sexual tension so thick between them she could almost bite into it as she would the succulent flesh of a juicy peach. She licked her lips.

"We might be strangers, Ruthie, but we're also lovers."

Lovers. Strangers. So contradictory. So true. The need grew stronger, deeper, making her body feel hot and limp, a mix of pleasure and aching emptiness that was almost painful.

"The Kerrigan is just a building," he said softly as he leaned closer, obviously about to kiss her.

Lethargic lust turned to flaming anger with frightening speed. Ruthie abruptly turned so his lips landed on the side of her head. Rigid with fury, she grabbed a butcher knife from the block on the counter, and centered it over the kiwi fruit sitting on the cutting board. "It is *not* just a building," she said before sending the knife through the fruit with a firm flick of her wrist. It made a loud thwacking sound as the metal blade struck the wood cutting board, neatly cutting the kiwi in half. "And there is *nothing* going on between us!" She punctuated that remark by chopping the second kiwi.

His gulp and step back gave her a moment of satisfaction. She was reaching for the banana when he threw his hands up into the air. "Uncle," he said with a chuckle. "Please don't make me watch while you hack that up."

"You're free to leave anytime."

He sighed. "All right, Ruthie, obviously I shouldn't have ambushed you here, in your own home, at this time of night. But we do need to talk. Soon. I'll be in town for the rest of the week and I hope you'll meet with me, privately, so we can clear the air."

"What else needs to be said?" she asked, her voice shaky.

"A lot. Last night wasn't a one-night stand for me, no matter what you think. And this problem between us isn't insurmountable."

"It's six stories high," Ruthie mumbled.

He reached for her, running his fingers across the side of her cheek. She pulled away, unwilling to be touched, cajoled, or seduced out of her righteous anger.

"I used to pretend I was a superhero when I was a kid," he said gently.

Ruthie scowled. "Well, how's your x-ray vision? Can you look into my mind and see what I'm thinking of you right now?"

His seductive chuckle made her wonder if he really had sneaked into her mind and found the lustful little thoughts hiding away in there behind the anger. She narrowed her eyes, forcing herself to think of adequate torture methods to deal with the man.

"I think I've got an idea of what's on your mind, sweetheart," he said with a grin. "But even if my x-ray vision's not the greatest, I've got a keen sense of smell. And right now I smell burning nuts."

She gasped. Then, glancing at the toaster oven,

Ruthie muttered a curse as she realized he was not kidding. She pulled out the tray, noting this batch of almonds, too, was beyond salvage. "I should give up and go to bed," she muttered eyeing the browned mess.

"I'm sorry, Ruthie," Robert said in complete seriousness as he walked across the kitchen toward the doorway. She saw a warning twinkle in his eye. "As much as I appreciate the invitation, I didn't come over here to go to bed with you tonight. I just wanted to talk."

He didn't duck fast enough to avoid the banana she sent flying across the room.

RUTHIE GOT a grand total of four hours sleep that night. Robert had left after the banana careened off his right shoulder, though the laughter in his eyes had lingered in her mind long after he'd gone. As had the memory of his hands. The thought of his kiss. What little sleep she'd had was restless, filled with erotic dreams that left her shaking when she woke.

Getting up early the next morning, as was her custom, Ruthie spent a few hours cleaning her apartment. Busy hands, she figured, would mean no time for thinking. Wrong. Now that Robert Kendall had been in her apartment, it was too easy to picture him standing in the doorway, or on the chair waving madly at the smoke detector with a towel. Worse was the memory of him pressing close to her in the kitchen so that the room receded and all she could see was his large, hard body.

Hoping for any distraction, she called the restaurant to tell the day staff what she wanted ordered from the produce delivery service. She also reiterated how long the quiche she'd prepared the weekend before should be thawed, then baked, in order to ensure cleanly cut slices for this morning's breakfast crowd. The phone call wasn't necessary. The kitchen workers knew the routine.

Nor did it distract her from thoughts of Robert Kendall. "He's the enemy, Ruthie," she told herself as she scrubbed her kitchen floor, finding tiny pieces of burnt almond beneath the cabinets. "And even if he weren't, he's all wrong for you!"

He *was* all wrong for her. Driven, professional, success oriented, he simply didn't fit in with Ruthie's rosy plans for her future. Her dreams, for as long as she could remember, had involved family. Career, school, even the Kerrigan receded in importance when she thought of the one foremost goal of her life.

She wanted babies. Lots of babies. She'd hated growing up an only child, and never felt that void more keenly than the night her father had died. She wouldn't want a child of hers to experience such pain alone, without siblings to lean on.

Having children meant needing to choose the right father for them—a father who put his family life first. He'd work hard at his career because it enhanced the happiness of their home life, but would never let that career jeopardize that happiness. Robert definitely wouldn't meet that criteria. He was a workaholic who wanted to "take on the world." He'd said so himself.

Besides that, he'd come right out and proclaimed that he didn't even want children! He liked living alone, liked things clean, streamlined, uncluttered. Ruthie figured any kid of hers would be born with scabs on both knees and smudges of chocolate on each cheek. A trail of small dirty fingerprints trailing up a white wall beneath an unused banister probably wasn't Robert Kendall's idea of interior design. But it sounded heavenly to Ruthie.

When it came right down to it, he also didn't understand much of anything about the other thing Ruthie felt passionately about: family loyalty. If he had, he would never have been able to look in her face and say the Kerrigan was "just a building." It wasn't just a building, it was the Sinclair way of life. The Kerrigan was their dream and their past and their future. It was the glue that held the extended family together, where the young ones could laugh over the antics of the elderly, while always still respecting and loving them for their quirks and eccentricities. And where the elderly could share their knowledge and nod their heads wisely while pondering the foolish escapades of the young.

Ruthie wanted that for her children. She wanted it for herself.

None of which changed the fact that she still very much wanted *him*.

ROBERT WAS SITTING at a table in the restaurant having a late lunch when Ruthie arrived at work that afternoon. She didn't see him until after she entered—and after he saw her—so there was no chance of ducking back out to avoid him. Not that she would have! After all, this was her restaurant, no way was he going to force her out. Still, she moved quickly, skimming around tables in a direct path to the kitchen, not looking his way at all.

"Sleep well?" he asked, his voice carrying in the large, tile-floored room as she tried to walk past his table.

"Like a baby," she insisted sweetly, the lie not sticking in her throat a bit.

"I didn't. Funny how the bed in my suite seems so much bigger than the one in yours."

Ruthie's eyes narrowed. She glanced around to see if anyone had overheard. Luckily, the restaurant was not crowded, since it was midafternoon, after the lunch rush but before dinner. She was glad no one on her staff had been walking by at that particular moment. "What do you want?"

"I haven't looked at the menu yet."

Ruthie grabbed one out of the hands of a young man sitting at a nearby table, muttered an apology, and thrust it into Robert's face. "Here."

He grinned. "Maybe what I want isn't on the menu. Maybe I need something unique that only the chef can provide."

Ruthie sneered. "Unless you're talking about my specialty of the day, which is chicken and walnuts in a bourbon cream sauce, I'm afraid you're outta luck."

He grew serious. "All I want is to talk, Ruthie. I want to be alone with you so we can work this out."

She looked into his eyes, gauging his mood. He wasn't being flirtatious or playful. The slight smile playing about his full lips was gentle, not seductive. Well, he couldn't prevent that mouth from appearing seductive—but at least he didn't appear to be intentionally messing with her head by playing on her sexual reaction to him.

It didn't matter. Her sexual reaction to him had a life of its own. Even now, in a public place, it sparked, making her whole body tingle. The scent of his cologne, which she'd forever identify with him, filled her head. Her stare was drawn to his long, lean hands, lingering on those fingers that had touched her with such exquisite precision.

Be alone with him? She'd be better off alone in a cage with a ravenous tiger. "No, Robert. There's no point in us talking. We're only going to go around in circles."

"I like going around in circles," he said with a coaxing grin. "Did I ever tell you about the time I went on the Ferris wheel at the county fair thirty-seven times in one day?"

She chuckled against her better judgment. "Did you win a contest or a prize?"

"A week of house arrest when my mama found out why I was too sick to go to school the next day." He reached for her hand, taking it gently and smoothing her fingers with his own. "Talk to me, Ruthie. That's one thing we do so well together."

Ooooh, he's good. His innocent words sent a not-so-innocent image of what *else* they did so well together shooting through her brain. She had to reach for the curved back of a nearby chair for support. "I've got to go. I have to get ready for the dinner rush."

Robert cast a pointed look around the nearly empty restaurant. "Looks like you can spare a few minutes. Come on, Ruthie, five minutes. Tell me about yourself, where you went to school, what made you decide to become a chef, how the heck you thought up that fabulous cream cheese and peppercorn stuffed filet mignon I had for dinner the other night."

His fingers were twined with hers, and she glanced down at them, getting a flash of memory of their bodies wrapped around each other in a similar manner. His gentle smile, his easy way of talking about any subject, and his genuine interest in her were just as difficult to resist as they had been Sunday night when they'd met. The late afternoon sun slanting in from the nearby window lent a feeling of warmth and lazy gentleness to a situation she knew in her heart was dangerous. But she was still tempted to pull out the other chair at the small café-style table and sit across from him.

"Did you have lots of freckles when you were a kid?" he asked, obviously sensing she was about to relent. "Did you go to summer camp? Where'd you go on your first date? Come on, Ruthie, there's so much more to explore between us."

"Here," she mumbled.

"What?"

"My first date." She glanced around the restaurant, noting the changes the years had wrought, but still remembering how it had looked when she'd been a young girl of sixteen wearing a strapless peach gown sitting across from a boy in a dark blue suit. "Here. In this restaurant. Under the watchful eyes of my father and the family. We were going to the homecoming dance and we came here for dinner. To the Kerrigan."

Robert's smile faded. "The Kerrigan."

"Yes, Robert, the Kerrigan. It was about six months before my father died," she said staring him directly in the eye. "Are you starting to get it? Are you coming close to having an inkling of how devastating yesterday's board meeting was to me?"

"Ruthie, I..."

Ruthie felt tears rise to her eyes at the look of tender understanding on his face. She dashed them away angrily. She didn't want his tenderness, or his understanding. She just wished he would leave, better yet, wished he had never come, had never threatened her secure world, her sense of family, of history, even of self.

Then she paused. Wished he had never come? In the mental mirror in her brain, she looked at herself and said one word: *Liar.*

"I can't talk to you, Robert. Not now. Not later. Would you like me to send a waitress over to take your order?"

He seemed to sense the finality of her decision because the light suddenly faded from his eyes. "I'm sorry, Ruthie. I'm so damn sorry."

She weakened. Only a little, but enough to scare her. Without giving him another glance, she walked away.

7

A FEW HOURS LATER, after the first rush of early diners—mostly elderly visitors—had departed the restaurant, Ruthie decided to grab a quick break before the later crowd came in. It was after six, but she knew it would still be light enough to sit outside by the pool for a few minutes and enjoy the last rays of the setting sun. She needed to be alone, quiet, needed to calm her churning thoughts.

It hadn't been easy to go back to work, but she'd done it. She'd calmly prepared marinade, seasoned vegetables, made last-minute changes to the starch side dish for the evening because of an unexpected shortage of wild rice. And all the while her mind had been elsewhere. With him. In a darkened kitchen filled with laughter and champagne. In a darker bedroom filled with slick kisses and warm, dreamy caresses.

She badly needed some air. Leaving her assistant in charge for a few minutes, she left the restaurant, intending to go right outside. Before she could pass through the lobby, however, she spied Celeste emerging from the elevator. Most of the men in the vicinity stopped to watch her lovely, blond cousin, too. Ruthie hid a smile, knowing Celeste didn't even notice. Since meeting her new husband, Dain, last year, Celeste had been oblivious to every other man on the planet.

"What are you doing here?" Ruthie asked, intercepting her cousin before she reached the check-in desk. "You're supposed to be on your honeymoon!"

Celeste shrugged. "You think I was gonna be able to enjoy ten days of sun, sand, alcohol and great sex not knowing what was happening up here with the hotel?"

Ruthie tapped her finger against the side of her cheek, a smile tugging at her lips. "Well..."

Celeste laughed. "Okay, yeah, I guess I could have enjoyed it. But Dain promised me a rain check. He knows I would have been distracted and he's the one who suggested we put off our trip for a couple of weeks."

"He's a darling," Ruthie said. "I feel terrible that you're missing out on your vacation, though!"

"It's all right. We're staying here at the hotel for a few nights, so it's sort of like a holiday. Believe me, I'm getting some use out of that book you gave me at my wedding shower, the one about invitations for sex? We played strangers in a bar last night. I handed him our room key wrapped in a pair of red silk underwear."

Ruthie choked out a laugh. "Those room keys sure do get around," she mumbled under her breath. Her cousin looked at her quizzically, but she didn't try to explain.

"Walk with me to my office," Celeste said. "I've been tossing some figures around and I want to show them to you."

Glancing at her watch, Ruthie realized she had a little time to spare and followed Celeste. They were just rounding the corner beyond the lobby, heading toward the offices, when Ruthie spied a very tall, dark-haired man engaged in a heated conversation with a brunette.

"Celeste—wait a second!" she hissed.

Her cousin immediately stopped, followed her stare

and saw what had caught Ruthie's attention. She ducked back behind the corner with Ruthie. The two of them peered around the ivory-colored wallpaper to unabashedly eavesdrop on the conversation.

"Monica, why do we keep having this discussion? There's no reason for you to stay. The next few days involve critical meetings with the money guys, contractors and hotel management. If you're going to be as much of a liability as you were at yesterday's board meeting, I'd rather you go back to New York."

Ruthie could tell by the look of anger on the other woman's face that she wasn't pleased to be told to shut up and go home.

"I did nothing wrong at the meeting, I just told it like it is. You're the one who's seemed distracted since we got here."

Robert's shoulders tensed. Ruthie could see his suit jacket go tight against his flexed arms. "I'm focused on the goal," he said, his voice steady. "If you can focus on that, too, then fine, stay. In any case, at least try to avoid alienating the Sinclair family any more than you already have."

The woman shook her head and made a *tsk*ing sound. "My, you're testy today, Robert. Are you already regretting the way our late-night plans turned out Sunday night?"

Ruthie stiffened.

"Maybe the board meeting would have gone better yesterday," she continued, "if you'd spent the night before focusing on enjoyment, rather than sacrificing yourself on the altar of business trying to take over this old moldering ruin. A night in the *right* bed could have sweetened things up considerably."

Ruthie sucked in her breath, her eyes widening with

shock as she absorbed what the woman had said. Business? Robert had been focusing on business Sunday night?

Meeting her. Seducing her. *Business?*

"As I said," Robert finally replied, "mixing business and pleasure is a bad idea."

"Well, obviously you got no pleasure. So I hope you're happy being *stuck* with business."

The woman turned her back and walked away. Robert took off in the other direction, bursting through a back exit that led to the parking garage.

And Ruthie just shook.

"Well, what a charmer she is," Celeste muttered. Then she looked up and noticed the stricken expression Ruthie felt sure was on her face. "Honey, what's wrong?"

"I'm going to kill him," Ruthie said through teeth so tightly clenched her jaw hurt. She couldn't believe she'd wasted tears on this man! Wasted precious moments remembering a sensual interlude which had obviously meant nothing to him!

"Who?"

Feeling as if she might explode if she didn't get things off her chest, Ruthie answered. "Him. Robert Kendall. He used me. Stupid! How could I have been so stupid?" Frustration nearly caused her to bang her head on the wall.

Celeste didn't act confused or ask a bunch of pointless questions. "Spill it."

Ruthie looked around quickly to be certain they were alone. She spotted no one in this back hallway, but still leaned closer to ensure she wouldn't be overheard. "I'm business!" She tried to whisper, but the words were more like a wail.

A look of consternation crossed Celeste's face, then her eyes narrowed. "And you thought you were pleasure?"

Ruthie bit her lip and nodded, relieved Celeste was blessed with such intuition and intelligence.

"When?"

"Sunday night."

Ruthie quickly told her cousin everything that had happened after the wedding. She tried to omit the most intimate details. Considering the evening had been one entire intimate interlude, however, she wasn't able to leave much out.

"Damn, Ruthie, you had sex more times on my wedding night than I did!"

"Oh, please don't remind me," she said, not knowing whether to laugh or cry at her cousin's indignant expression. "It's too awful to remember."

"No good?"

Ruthie paused, looking at the other woman out of the corner of her eye. "Amazing."

"Amazing, huh?" her cousin said, a speculative look on her face. "Okay, maybe he's a snake, but I'm still glad you spent the night with him rather than the walking calculator."

"I thought you liked Bobby."

Celeste shrugged. "He's nice enough. But, remember your motto back in college when you first decided the time had come to lose your virginity?"

Ruthie chuckled, remembering coming home from school on holidays and telling Celeste, who'd been two years younger, all about her romantic adventures. "Yep. I was never going to go to bed with a guy who weighed less than I did. If he was skinny enough to fit into my jeans, he wasn't getting into my pants."

Celeste smirked. "Right. And, cute as he is, Bobby looks like a teenager. Now, as for Mr. Kendall...in spite of the lean hips and tight butt, I don't think that gorgeous man would be able to get even your retaining-water-and-bloated jeans up over those hard thighs."

"You've no idea," Ruthie murmured, visualizing his muscular legs entwined with her own in the hotel bed. She sighed as she glanced toward the exit through which Robert had left the building.

Straightening her shoulders, she shook off the dreamy memory. "That doesn't mean he's not a cockroach, however. You heard them. Obviously he set me up. Going to bed with me was part of his business plan for taking over the Kerrigan!"

Celeste shook her head slowly. "I don't think you can jump to that conclusion, Ruthie. How could he know you'd be in the kitchen? Or that you'd drop your key? Or that you'd take cold pills instead of aspirin?"

Her cousin made sense. There were too many variables for her to believe Robert had intentionally sought her out to seduce her.

Ruthie thought about it some more. "Well, maybe he didn't set out to go to bed with me. But he obviously talked to that woman all about it! Do you know how humiliating that is, knowing he's discussing my sex life?"

"As humiliating as it would be for him to know you're discussing *his* sex life?"

Ruthie shot Celeste a look of exasperation. "Must you always be right?"

Celeste grinned and gave a tiny bow. "I must."

Ruthie leaned against the wall, crossing her arms tightly in front of her chest. "It's not the same thing, anyway. I know I can trust you enough to tell you something this..."

"Deliciously sinful?" her cousin prompted.

"No. I was going to say this 'private.' I know you won't tell another living soul. But what about her?"

"You don't know that he told her anything."

Ruthie rolled her eyes. "You heard her. She told him he spent the other night in the wrong bed—obviously meaning *my* bed!"

"So? Look, Ruthie, maybe the best thing for you to do is to confront him about it. Ask him if he blabbed, and make sure that woman won't repeat anything."

Confront him? Intentionally seek him out? Ruthie shook her head. "Out of the question. I never want to see him again."

Her cousin's snort was short and inelegant. "Chicken."

"I'm not afraid," Ruthie retorted. "Nor am I stupid. That man gets to me, Celeste. If I give him the chance, he'll have me forgetting why he's here."

The two of them turned to walk down the back corridor toward the accounting offices. "It's gonna be okay, honey," Celeste said as she hooked her arm around Ruthie's waist.

"I don't see how," Ruthie mumbled. "A man I went to bed with wants to destroy my family. Robert Kendall is a shark. He slept with me, and now he's going to use my own feelings against me to get what he wants—the Kerrigan. I'd really like to make him pay. I wonder how he'd like Ex-Lax in his chocolate cake!"

Celeste laughed softly and gave her a squeeze. "Revenge ain't your style, kid."

"I'm entitled to fantasize." Hearing someone moving behind them, Ruthie stopped and quickly glanced over her shoulder. Her cousin Chuck had just stepped out of the men's room and was watching them with interest. Ruthie winced, wondering how much he'd heard. "Chuck?"

He didn't answer right away. His bright blue eyes were narrowed, and an unfamiliar look of concentration was evident on his handsome, tanned face. Suddenly, noticing Ruthie and Celeste watching him, he shook his head and smiled his vacant grin. "Hey, Sinclairs. I mean, Sinclair and...oh, man, what's your new name again, Celly?"

"It's Underwood," Celeste said. "And don't call me Celly."

Ruthie saw Celeste grin, and knew she was thinking the same thing—Chuck obviously hadn't heard, or didn't understand the implication of their conversation.

"Hey, why is it you two grew up and got to be Chuck and Celeste, and I'm still stuck with Ruthie?"

"Don't blame me," Chuck said. "I thought I'd be Chuckie forever until that cool movie came out with the redheaded doll who went around killing everybody. That's when Mom decided I needed to be Chuck."

"Pray to Wes Craven," Celeste said with a grin. "Maybe he'll make a film about an ax murderer named Ruthie."

Ruthie paused, pursing her lips thoughtfully. "You know, I could probably come up with a great first victim."

ROBERT HAD intentionally spent the afternoon out of the hotel following his conversation with Ruthie. She needed a break—from him, from the situation. While

her anger hadn't dissuaded him, the tears he'd felt sure
he'd seen sparkling on her lashes had. It was tough
backing off, giving her time. But he had to do it. Ruthie
had to sort it out and come to the realization that he
wasn't her enemy. Once she accepted that, he looked
forward to proving just how much more he could be to
her.

So he'd gone out, done the tourist bit in Philadelphia, though it bored him to tears. He'd even grabbed
a burger at a drive-through on the way back to the hotel that evening, wanting to avoid going into her restaurant. Ruthie probably would have tried to poison
him, anyway. "Nah, not her style. Ruthie's more a
stomp-on-the-foot kind of woman," he'd told himself.
The thought had made him smile.

The argument he'd had with Monica when he'd gotten back to the Kerrigan around dinnertime had left
him frustrated and angry. Needing to pound something, he'd spent a couple of hours working out in the
fitness center downstairs.

Though it was now nearly ten, Robert felt drained
and sweaty after the workout, and decided to take a
shower. When he got back to his room, he ignored the
flashing message light on the phone, figuring Monica
was the one calling.

Stripping off his stale clothes, he dropped them on
the bed, and went into the bathroom. He took a long,
hot shower, enjoying the feel of the pulsing jets of water on the tight muscles of his back.

It was only when he heard a loud knock coming
from the door that he turned off the water. There was
only one person who'd be coming to see him at this
time of night—Monica.

Though he thought about avoiding her, he figured

she'd only keep pounding. Thrusting back the shower curtain, Robert reached toward the towel rack.

Empty. There were no towels. Disbelieving, he looked all around the bathroom. Not a single scrap of terry cloth was in sight—not even a washcloth to mop up the water dripping in his eyes. "Dammit," he muttered, cursing a forgetful maid.

The knocking didn't let up. Frustrated, annoyed, and soaking wet, Robert ran his palms over his arms and legs, trying to brush off as much water as he could. "Hold on a minute!" he yelled, prepared to bite Monica's head off as soon as he found clothes to pull on.

He strode out of the room naked, nearly slipping on the wet tile, which set off another string of curses. He'd just reached the door when the knock came again. Luckily, the room was equipped with a peephole. He looked out, fully expecting to see his boss's daughter, but instead saw a mass of red curls. "Ruthie?"

She was biting her lip in indecision. As he watched, she turned, as if about to walk away. Glancing around frantically for something to wear, he grabbed the first thing he could reach—a white handkerchief lying with his wallet and keys on a nearby table. It didn't cover much. He yanked the door open anyway. "Ruthie! I'm here!"

Hearing Robert's call, Ruthie turned around. And froze. "Are you crazy?" she asked, casting a quick glance in either direction to see if anyone else was sharing the view of the nearly naked man standing in the doorway.

"Oh, my goodness," she whispered, unable to look away from the bare, three-mile-wide, masculine chest. Her lips parted as she struggled to find air. Ruthie curled her fingers, not even conscious she was doing it, remembering the feel of that dark, crisp hair that was sprinkled over his taut, tanned skin, and on down his rippled belly.

His hips were lean, his thighs tight and muscular, covered with more of that sexy dark hair. Ruthie leaned against the nearest wall, banging her elbow on the metal edge of the fire extinguisher but not caring in the least.

Raising her stare up his body, she saw water dripping down his corded neck. It was physically impossible for her to pull her attention away from a drop that slid from his collarbone across one flat male nipple, over the plane of his stomach and the line of his hip. She bit the corner of her mouth, trying to hold in a sigh.

"You're dripping," she whispered, knowing if she stood here staring at him for another ten seconds she'd be able to say the same thing about herself. She immediately straightened and turned toward the elevator.

"Don't leave!" he ordered. "Please, Ruthie."

She paused to glare at him over her shoulder. "You're practically stark naked!"

As if he was just realizing it himself, he quickly looked down, then adjusted the thin—*very* thin—handkerchief, which he held across his hips with his flattened forearm. Ruthie was half-tempted to ask him to take his arm away, willing to lay money that gravity wasn't taking that white cotton square anywhere!

She closed her eyes and crossed her arms. Tapping her foot on the carpeted floor of the corridor, she hissed, "Get dressed." Looking at him, to see if he was going to obey, she saw his look of worry. "I'll wait here," she promised.

"You'll leave."

"No," she said, knowing she was crazy not to do exactly that. But it had taken a lot for her to work up the nerve to try calling him earlier and to make this quick trip up to his room to confront him about his conversation with Monica Winchester. She wasn't going to back down now in spite of his...his...yumminess.

"I came up here to talk to you. That's what I plan to do."

He didn't look like he believed her. Just then, a door across the hall opened, and Ruthie saw the night-cream-smeared face of an elderly woman peeking through the crack left between the chain and the door frame. The woman's eyes widened into twin spotlights. Ruthie could have sworn a very low, shaky wolf whistle emanated from her pursed, wrinkled lips.

"Get in here!" Robert growled, grabbing Ruthie's arm. She nearly flew off her feet as he tugged her into his room.

Before she could protest, he'd pushed the door shut behind her. "Now, stay here. Don't go anywhere."

Ruthie had to try very hard to keep a straight face as he backed away from her. She saw him cast a quick glance toward the bed. He snagged a pair of gym shorts—nothing else—and continued backing toward the bathroom.

"Don't hit the...ouch," she mumbled in sympathy as she saw him bang the back of his leg on the edge of a chair. "You okay?"

He winced. "Don't leave!"

Kicking at the door with the heel of his foot, he backed into the bathroom. Ruthie had one quick, completely gratuitous—completely delicious—view of his taut backside in the steamed mirror before he pushed the door shut.

Ruthie crossed her arms, trying to regain her composure, which had evaporated in the moments since he'd answered the door. It had taken Ruthie an hour of mental arguing to make the mountainous three-story journey in the hotel elevator to confront him. But she'd had to do it.

It was bad enough knowing Robert had the knowledge of their amazing night together to hold over her head. The possibility that Monica Winchester did, too, was too much to bear. She needed to know, one way or another. That need outweighed everything, her embarrassment, even her anger. She didn't know, however, if it outweighed the lust that was shooting through her body, leaving her so weak-legged she thought she'd have to sink to the bed.

Before she had time to do anything, he was back out of the bathroom. "Okay, I'm decent now."

He had been a whole lot more than decent before!

He was still very distracting, clad only in a pair of black nylon shorts that clung to his still-wet body. She had to stare at her own fingers, pretending to check a chipped nail, to keep from looking at him. "Couldn't you have even wrapped a towel around yourself before you answered the door?"

"I had no towels! Not one." Robert rolled his eyes. "The service in this place is outstanding."

Ruthie was surprised that one of their housekeepers had left the room inadequately supplied, but she wasn't about to admit that to him. She wasn't interested in discussing the Kerrigan with him at all!

"So, you've decided to talk to me, now?" he asked as he crossed the room to stand next to her...and next to the huge king-size bed.

She stepped away, sitting on a chair nearby, knowing there was no way in heck she was going to sit with him on the bed.

He sat down opposite her. "Does this mean you're going to listen to reason and you understand that this situation with the hotel is not my fault?"

"No, it doesn't. It means I overheard your conversation with your business associate downstairs this evening and I want to know just how much you told her about...about..."

"Us?"

Ruthie gave a noncommittal shrug and strove to sound casual. "About our accidental little sexual encounter."

He snorted a laugh. "Maybe accidental. Definitely not little."

She glared at him. "All right, our completely regrettable, reckless, crazy sexual encounter!"

"Reckless? Possibly. Crazy? Oh yeah, but only in the best way." His voice was playful, his tone seductive and intimate. Then he grew serious. "Regrettable? Not on your life."

His intensity unnerved her. She had to force herself to remember her reason for coming to talk to him. "You didn't answer my question."

"What was the question again?"

She let out an impatient sigh. "Did you or did you not tell your *business associate*, Monica Winchester, the daughter of the man trying to steal this hotel, that you and I slept together Sunday night?"

He grinned. "What're you, nuts? I don't kiss and tell, sugar—that's strictly high school."

Ruthie couldn't meet his eye, remembering the intimate details she'd shared with her cousin Celeste. She mumbled, "It sure sounded like she knew something."

"The only thing she knew," Robert explained, leaning forward to gently tug Ruthie's hand into his, "is that I didn't come to her room and sleep with her like she wanted me to. I spent a glorious, amazing night with you, which I would love the opportunity to repeat someday, after you decide you can trust me again."

His gentle tone and the sweet expression on his face masked the meaning of his words for about ten seconds. Then Ruthie erupted. "You were supposed to go to her room? You were supposed to sleep with her?"

Robert could have ripped his tongue out of his own head for putting it the way he had, because obviously Ruthie had misunderstood. She leapt out of her chair, her eyes flashing with fury. He quickly held up his hands to try to halt her eruption. "No, Ruthie, don't get the wrong idea."

"Well what is the right idea? Did she expect you to show up and *do* her or not?"

He winced at her crudity. "What she expected and what was actually going to happen are two different things."

As gently as possible, Robert explained exactly what had taken place in the hotel bar Sunday night. Ruthie listened, though she wouldn't sit back down. She stalked back and forth in the room, as if marching in a confined cell. But she listened.

"So you're saying Monica slipped you a condom and her room key, and you used the key only to tell her you weren't interested? Yeah, right. Tell me another one, Mr. Clinton!"

He stood, stopping her relentless march, holding her shoulders so she'd have to look at him. "It's true, Ruthie. The only reason I was going to her room that night was to clear the air so she wouldn't go into the board meeting the next day and ruin it. Which is exactly what she did!"

She looked confused, like part of her wanted to believe him, but she was scared to.

"I give you my word, Ruthie. Even if I hadn't met you I would never have gone to bed with Monica Winchester. Whether her father wants us together or not."

She looked at him like he was an idiot. "Well, gee, Mr. Corporate America, did you ever stop to wonder about her little present to you? If Daddy wants the two of you together, and she knows you're not taking her seriously, didja ever stop to think the whole thing might have been a setup?"

Robert didn't follow her.

She sighed in exasperation. "The old needle through the condom trick, pal, ever heard of it?"

Robert felt the blood rush from his face as he realized what she was talking about. "She wouldn't."

"Stranger things have been known to happen," Ruthie said. "If you're the golden boy, and she's the princess, and you two hooking up would make the old boy happy as a lark before he decides how to split up his millions in his will, maybe, just maybe, she would!"

Ruthie seemed to realize what she was saying. Suddenly, her own face went deadly pale. "Oh, my God, and we used that condom, didn't we!"

He paused, staring at her. "Don't think that way. I'm sure there was nothing wrong with it."

She wasn't listening. She resumed her stalking around the room, talking to herself, as if anticipating a future calamity.

He watched her for a minute, then planted himself directly in her path. "Ruthie, stop it! You're borrowing trouble."

"What if I'm pregnant? Huh? What then? Boy, talk about a bad girl. That'll win me the Sinclair Scarlet Woman prize hands down! Sex with a stranger and a baby with no father!"

He laughed through his frustration. "Do you write tragic novels in your other life? Where do you get this stuff?"

She suddenly looked at her own hands. "Are you saying it's impossible? That you can't, I mean, that I couldn't, uh, you said you don't want kids, have you been, uh...."

Her confusion was charming but he still winced at the image. "No, I haven't been 'fixed.' And yeah, I guess technically you could be pregnant. But do I really think you are? That Monica sabotaged a condom? No."

"But she might have!" Ruthie wailed.

Sensing she was about to resume her frantic pacing, Robert reacted impulsively. Grabbing her by the shoulders, he spun her around. Her eyes widened in shock, but he paid no attention. When she opened her mouth to protest, he caught her lips with his own, kissing her before he even knew he was going to do it.

Then everything else just disappeared. She was in his arms, her lips were so sweetly clinging to his, and...oh, he hadn't imagined it. He hadn't dreamed it. Kissing her was pleasure beyond description.

He heard her little sigh of acceptance and suddenly she went pliant and yielding in his arms. She slid her hands up over his shoulders and wrapped them around his neck, pulling him tighter. Tilting her head, she parted her lips. Robert licked them gently before slipping his tongue between to catch hers in a slow tango of dips and swirls in which no one led and no one followed. They both simply danced.

This time there was no chocolate. No champagne. Only sweet, beautiful, wonderful Ruthie with her hot, wet mouth and her seductive scent and her soft, curvy body pressing tightly against him. Robert remembered, then, what it was like to completely lose himself in another person. He'd experienced it before. With her. Just two nights ago.

Ruthie hadn't been prepared for the kiss. Nor, however, had she fought it. When he'd taken her in his arms, she knew he was trying to calm her down, to shut her up. She didn't care. His lips were firm, demanding, and his mouth tasted finer than anything she'd imagined. And she'd been imagining quite a lot since their dreamy night together.

She arched into him, digging her hands into the taut muscles of his shoulders, then sliding her palm down the smooth, hot skin of his back. He stiffened in her arms. Then he stiffened against her belly. His hot, heavy erection pressed through the nylon shorts as if there were no barrier between them at all, and Ruthie welcomed it, pressed against it, wishing she could feel flesh against flesh.

As if they had a life of their own, her hands slid lower, teasing the elastic waistband of his shorts, and she heard him groan. When he reached for her blouse, she didn't protest. Feeling like she was outside herself, watching someone else experience such pleasure, she kept kissing him, mindless of his fingers slipping free the top buttons to reveal the curves of her breasts. When he stroked her there, following the indentation of her cleavage, she leaned back, offering him greater access.

They fell to the bed.

And Ruthie woke up. "No!" She bounced back up off the mattress so fast, she probably looked like someone playing leapfrog. "This is *not* happening!"

He rolled onto his back, putting both hands over his eyes. Ruthie cast one quick glance at him, smothering a groan as she noted the tent in his shorts. She walked toward the door.

"Not. Happening."

Buttoning her blouse with hands that shook as if she'd lifted weights for an hour, Ruthie hurried out of the room.

8

IT TOOK ROBERT about twenty-four hours to realize he was the victim of sabotage. It dawned on him as soon as he got into bed the following night and felt the scratchy bare mattress beneath his feet. "Short-sheeted," he said with a sigh. Not quite believing it, he reluctantly flipped on the light, got out of bed and pulled off the quilted spread.

"Yep." He hadn't been short-sheeted since his college dorm days. Groaning, Robert yanked the linens off the bed and began to remake it. "Sabotage."

The towel incident should have been a tip-off. He didn't think there had ever been a time when he'd stayed in a decent hotel that took every single towel—including the *clean* ones—and didn't leave replacements. But he'd been distracted from the issue by Ruthie's completely unexpected arrival the night before. "Nice distraction, though," he admitted aloud.

He hadn't thought too much about the towels once Ruthie had stormed out of his room, taking her sweet, warm, willing little body with her. He'd been just a little preoccupied. It had taken thirty minutes to get over his urge to go after her, seduce her into coming back to his room and make love to her for hours. When he'd finally been able to move again, he'd called down to the front desk to request a wake-up call. Though nearly eleven, he'd informed the gum-chewing night clerk about the absence of towels in his room, and asked that fresh ones be brought up. He'd been assured they would be. And they had. Two hours later. *After* he'd given up and gone to bed.

Robert should have thoroughly chewed out the person who'd woken him up with the knock minutes after he'd fallen asleep, but couldn't muster the energy. He'd grabbed the two measly towels and slammed the door in the guy's face. Now he knew the late-night delivery was another example of sabotage.

And of course, this morning, there had been no wake-up call. Without it, he'd slept right through a breakfast meeting he'd arranged with a sales rep from a local contracting firm. The company wanted to pitch their abilities to renovate the Kerrigan, should the Winchester Corporation succeed in their takeover, which seemed almost beyond question. The salesman had finally called Robert's room, waking him up at around ten. He hadn't slept so late in years. But considering the long, sleepless nights he'd had ever since arriving in Philadelphia, he supposed it wasn't too surprising.

There had been a few glares from hotel staff when he'd walked through the lobby that afternoon. They hadn't come from Ruthie, who he'd never seen. He'd even had dinner in the restaurant, hoping to catch a glimpse of her. No such luck. She was obviously avoiding him. After their kiss in his room the night before, he thought he understood why. If she was as confused by what was happening between them as he was, she probably needed time to think it all through.

Attraction. Desire. Passion. Hell, be honest, mind-blowing lust. Yes, all of the above roared to life between them whenever they were in the same damn room.

But it went beyond that. Genuine liking. True appreciation for her zany spirit and sense of humor. A desire to sit and talk to her for hours, like they had the night they'd met. The realization when she'd started flipping out about defective condoms the night before that he hadn't been absolutely horrified. What the hell did all that mean?

He didn't know. He just knew he'd thought about it all day. Thought about her. Himself. His past. Maybe even a little bit about his future, which was downright nuts considering he'd known the woman for less than a week.

That didn't stop the fantasies niggling at the edges of his brain. Robert had to forcibly thrust them away as he wearily remade the bed, trying to work up some indignation toward the staff of the Kerrigan Towers Hotel for this latest act of terrorism.

When he'd come back to his room earlier that evening, he'd noted that there were towels in the bathroom. But, of course, no soap. Not even a single sliver left disintegrating on the side of the tub. He'd had the last laugh, however, since he generally had a spare bar floating around in his shaving kit. So the staff hadn't been able to make him too miserable today.

Until now. Short-sheeted. Robert had to chuckle. It was obvious the staff had gotten wind of the pending takeover, and they were acting on their displeasure. Not surprising. They'd probably become used to a laid-back managerial atmosphere and felt threatened by the idea of change. He could only assume the entire staff thought of the Kerrigan as a family establishment and were defending the Sinclairs. He liked that—liked the staff's loyalty, even if it was to a family who didn't know how to manage the financial side of a business.

When they realized how generous the Winchester Corporation could be to its employees, however, he felt sure they'd come around. In the meantime, he'd have to deal with these minor inconveniences. No towels or soap, slow service, poorly made beds. No big deal.

He wondered if Monica was receiving the same treatment, and, if so, how she was reacting to it. Since he'd managed to avoid her all day, he didn't know. But, given Monica's abilities to tick people off even when she wasn't trying to, it wouldn't be surprising if the annoyed staff tried to get even with her as well.

He also wondered what else the staff had in store for him. But having been raised with five brothers who had tormented him all his life, he figured he could take it. No way were they going to get rid of him, of course—even if he didn't have his business with the hotel to deal with. Now, more importantly, he had some personal business with Ruthie. He wasn't going anywhere.

THOUGH RUTHIE HAD managed to duck out of sight every time she'd spotted Robert the day before, on Thursday morning she smashed right into him. She'd been hurrying, as usual, running late for breakfast with Aunts Flossie and Lila. They came into the city every Thursday for their weekly doctor visits, and insisted that Ruthie meet them for gossip and feminine commiseration at least twice a month. Ruthie had given up asking them why they felt it necessary to see their doctor every single week. Knowing he was a widower, at least as old as they were, and very attentive to them, she had a feeling she didn't want to know the answer.

She'd just entered the hotel and turned sharply to the left toward the restaurant when she literally bumped into Robert Kendall. He'd been occupying her every waking thought anyway, especially after their kiss, so she couldn't say she was entirely shocked to see him. Not shocked. But not happy, either. "You!"

"You could have just asked me if I wanted to have breakfast with you," Robert said with a grin, "rather than body-slamming me toward the restaurant."

"Don't flatter yourself. I am having breakfast with my great-aunts."

"The two nutty old ladies?"

The grin on his lips let her know he was teasing, but Ruthie still frowned. "Don't talk about my family that way."

"Sorry, I wasn't trying to pick a fight," he said. "I guess I'm used to my own more eccentric relatives and didn't figure you'd be so...sensitive...about yours."

Ruthie put a fist on her hip. "I'm not sensitive. And you didn't say 'the two eccentric old ladies'—you used the word nutty."

"Touché. So how are the *eccentric* femme fatale and the kleptomaniac?"

The teasing look he gave her out of the corner of his eye brought a sudden laugh to Ruthie's lips. "You noticed?"

"Uh, yeah. Remind me never to be sitting behind your Aunt Flossie when she decides she wants her dinner plate—and flings her meal over her shoulder."

"Bless her heart, she truly is a darling," Ruthie said. "She doesn't really steal things, you know."

Robert raised an eyebrow and gave her a look of disbelief.

"No, I mean it. She just borrows," Ruthie explained. "Aunt Flossie went through a very bad time during the Depression as a runaway teenage bride. And as she's gotten older, she worries about every penny. So she, uh, picks up things, then wraps them up and gives them back to people, as gifts."

Robert's shoulders shook as he chuckled. "So, I guess that means your uncle's going to get his gold pen back?"

"I'm sure he already has."

The moment of shared humor left Ruthie with a strange feeling in her stomach. His grin was genuine and charming, his brown eyes sparkling with amusement. It had felt like this that first night, Sunday night. She'd wondered in the past few days when things had gone so crazy if she'd imagined how easy it had been to talk to him, laugh with him. She hadn't. She was every bit as attracted to him now as she'd been the moment they met. No, *more* attracted, because now she knew how it felt to be in his arms, to feel his lips on hers and his hands on her skin. Though she still couldn't remember everything from Sunday night, some of the gaps in her memory had been filled in by the reality of their subsequent embrace in his room.

Needing to get away from him now, before her defenses crumbled around her any more than they already had, Ruthie stepped away. "I've got to go."

He held an arm in front of her, blocking her path. Ruthie glanced around, seeing the curious stares of some other people walking by to enter the restaurant. "Wait. Please, give me a minute to talk to you."

"There's nothing left to say."

"We didn't exactly finish our...conversation...the other night."

She snorted. "Conversation. Is that what you call it?"

"No, what I call it is lovemaking, and we didn't finish that, either."

Her eyes widening, Ruthie took another quick look around, hoping no one she knew had overheard. "It should never have happened. Not Tuesday night. Not Sunday night."

"But it did, Ruthie. It did, and I'd be a liar if I said I regretted it. So what do I have to do to make you admit you feel the same way?"

She thought about it for less than a heartbeat. "Give up your plans to take over the Kerrigan."

He sighed. "It's not that simple, Ruthie."

"Sure it is. Tell your boss it's a bad move and walk away. I'm sure he'd listen to you." Ruthie didn't mean to plead with him. She'd had no intention of asking him to do such a thing, but he'd presented her with the opportunity. As usual, she said what was in her heart, not letting her head interfere too much with her tongue. The words were there now, hanging between them, and it was up to him to make the next move.

She knew what he'd say.

"I can't do that."

Ruthie ducked under his arm, but again he blocked her path, saying, "You are asking me to betray my principles."

She held his eye. "And you're asking me to watch while you betray my family."

He stepped back, dropping his arm to let her pass, and nodded his head. "Then I suppose we're at an impasse."

Ruthie saw the sadness on his face, and it got to her. Whatever else the man had said or done, she had to admit he'd tried. He'd felt the amazing emotional tug-of-war going on between them, and he'd tried to give them a chance to see where it would lead. But she couldn't back down.

"It doesn't matter, Robert," she said regretfully. "Even if the six stories of the Kerrigan weren't standing between us, we are still completely different people. My loyalty is to family, to tradition, to memories. And yours is to your boss and your career and your rosy, affluent, *solitary* future."

He didn't deny it.

And this time, when she walked away, he didn't stop her.

LATE THAT NIGHT, when the restaurant was closed and the kitchen cleaned and quiet, Ruthie sat with the assistant manager, going over food orders for the following week. She'd had a long, miserable day, haunted by the tenderness in Robert's eyes when he'd finally given up on her for good.

Ruthie had spent the day second-guessing her decision to turn her back on him—on them. She wondered if there would come a time when she would seriously regret not exploring the heady, turbulent, emotionally thrilling relationship she sensed they could have together. She somehow thought she'd already reached that moment.

"Ruthie, you here?"

Looking up, she saw Tina, the bubbly blond desk clerk, enter through the quiet, darkened restaurant. Tina nodded to the assistant manager, who gathered her belongings and left for the night.

"Got any snacks lying around?" Tina asked. "You still owe me some key lime pie."

Ruthie grinned. "Here. Help yourself," she said as

she opened the refrigerator where they kept all the cold desserts.

"Yes!" Tina muttered. The girl was reaching for a foil-covered pie when Ruthie saw something jiggle in the lower leg pocket of her loose khaki painter pants. "What on earth is that moving around in your pocket?" she asked, not sure she really wanted to know.

Tina immediately crouched down to poke a finger at something that looked suspiciously like a furry white face. "Get back in there!"

"Tina? You want to explain why you're carrying a live creature in your pants?"

The girl's pretty blue eyes widened, the whites nearly glowing in the dimly lit kitchen. "Uh...it's just Max."

"Max?"

"My rat."

Ruthie gave a little screech and dropped her pen. She resisted the ingrained impulse to climb up on top of the table and scream hysterically at the idea of a rodent within a hundred yards. "A rat? You brought a *rat* into my kitchen? What are you trying to do, get the Health Department to shut us down?"

Tina stepped back. "Gee, no, Ruthie. He's my pet, he's cute and white and fuzzy with the most adorable long pink tail."

Ruthie felt nauseous. "I *hate* rats. Especially in my kitchen!"

"I'm sorry. I didn't even think about that. I kinda forgot he was in there, I guess he's been sleeping."

Forget about a rat in her pocket? Ruthie didn't think she could forget seeing a rat from a mile away. "Why on earth would you bring a rodent to work with you?"

The girl looked around nervously, like a cornered...well, like someone caught in an uncomfortable situation. "Tina?"

"It's a joke, a trick we were going to play."

"We?"

"Me and some of the other employees," the girl muttered.

Ruthie saw the little face come poking up, pushing at the snap holding Tina's pants pocket closed. She covered her eyes and groaned. "Oh, please get that thing out of here."

Tina turned and quickly walked toward the kitchen exit. "Sorry. I'll come back another night."

"I mean get it out of the hotel, Tina!" Ruthie called as the girl slipped into the darkened restaurant. Then, just before Tina could leave, Ruthie walked after her. "Wait a second. Who exactly were you playing this joke on?"

Tina paused at the door that led from the restaurant to the lobby and grinned over her shoulder. "Oh, that hunky corporate creep. The guy trying to take over the Kerrigan. We've been making his stay a little less than comfortable."

Ruthie gasped. "Robert Kendall? You're not serious! What have you done to him?"

Tina must have seen the dismay on Ruthie's face, in spite of the dark and shadowed room, because her only answer was a helpless shrug and a guilty grin. She quickly pushed the door open and exited before Ruthie could question her further.

Ruthie shook her head, unable to believe what Tina had let slip. The staff had been doing things to make one of their guests uncomfortable? Never mind that the guest was a shark waiting for them to flounder so he could gobble up the Kerrigan. He was still a paying

guest in their hotel and Ruthie was aghast that he'd
been treated less than cordially.

"The towels," she mumbled aloud, knowing they'd
been intentionally forgotten as part of some crazy "get
even" plan. And what a mess *that* prank had caused! If
she hadn't seen him all wet and dripping and delicious, she would never have ended up in his arms.
Well, okay, it hadn't happened just because of the impossibly wide chest, bare and glistening with water, or
the ripple of muscle in his arms. Or that tiny white cotton handkerchief. She closed her eyes, shivering at *that*
mental picture.

If she was going to be honest with herself she'd have
to admit the towels had nothing to do with the fact that
she'd ended up in his arms again. She'd gone to his
room of her own free will. The overwhelming attraction between them had sparked into a conflagration
when he'd kissed her. And she'd wanted him to. That's
all. Towels or no towels. Luscious bare skin or no luscious bare skin. She wanted him. Still.

"Which is why you need to stay away from him, Sinclair," she told herself as she went back into the kitchen
to finish doing some paperwork.

Tomorrow was Friday, the beginning of another
busy weekend, and there would be no time for order-
ing, planning specials, or looking at menu options for
the next few days. But the thought of what Tina had
told her wouldn't leave her alone. She should have
stopped the girl from leaving, should have demanded
details. What on earth had they been doing to him?
Some of the hotel's employees had been around longer
than Ruthie had, so she knew their loyalty ran deep.
Deep enough to do something really stupid? Or even
dangerous?

Tomorrow she'd bring the situation to her uncle Henry's attention, and he'd put an immediate stop to it. No one would be fired, she was sure. Henry's kindness and generosity toward the hotel employees was probably one of the reasons the Kerrigan was in such a poor financial situation. He was generous to a fault, forgiving and trusting. A soft touch and the kind of man who truly believed in the goodness of other people. Sometimes his gentle smile seemed so much like her father's that it brought tears to Ruthie's eyes.

Yes, Uncle Henry could deal with it tomorrow.

But what about tonight?

She couldn't stop worrying about it. About him— Robert. Before she thought better of it, Ruthie found herself crossing to the small office behind the kitchen, where she never worked since it was stacked high with cartons and boxes. But there was also an in-house phone buried under all the supplies. Before she could change her mind, she reached out and picked it up.

WORKING ON HIS laptop in his room, Robert was deep in concentration. He'd been communicating with the home office by e-mail and fax all week, and had talked to James Winchester on the phone that afternoon. Now there were reports and letters to write, figures to go over. He didn't mind the late work hours. It was a distraction from the silence of the lonely room.

The sudden jarring double-ring of the phone on the bedside table startled him. He glanced at his watch, noting the late hour. When he answered the phone and heard Ruthie's voice, he couldn't believe it. "Ruthie? Is everything okay?"

"Look, I'm sorry to bother you, but I just learned something you ought to know about."

Robert listened while Ruthie told him about the staff's intention to make his visit to the Kerrigan Towers less than pleasant. When she told him about the worker with the white rat in her pocket, Robert laughed out loud. "A rat? That's unique. But what was the plan? Was I supposed to get the message that I was being called a rat or be so repulsed I'd leave immediately? Or maybe think the building was a lot worse off than I'd thought and give up the takeover plans?"

"Hm. Not a bad idea," she said with a sly chuckle. "Anyway, I wanted to warn you. I'm sure my uncle will deal with it in the morning. But, you might want to be careful tonight."

"I don't know. You've got me pretty nervous now. Maybe you should come up to my room and check me...it...out?"

She giggled. "That was pretty lame."

"I know," he said with a soft laugh. Then he grew serious. "Come anyway, Ruthie. Come." He heard her shaky sigh and knew she'd heard the blatant sensuality of his suggestion. And he didn't care in the least.

She ignored it. "I'm sure everything will be fine."

Sensing she was about to hang up, Robert quickly asked, "Where are you?"

"Why?" She sounded suspicious, on guard.

"Just wondering."

She didn't answer his question. "Look, I have to get going. I'm sorry I called so late."

She hung up before he could say a word. Robert placed the receiver back in its cradle. He glanced thoughtfully at the phone, remembering the distinctive double-ring. A second later, it clicked. "She's downstairs."

He shouldn't. He knew he shouldn't, especially after

the conversation they'd had outside the restaurant that morning. She wanted him to leave her alone. That's exactly what he should do, go back to work, forget about her call, then get some sleep. But the thought of another long restless night in the large bed was not particularly appealing. Especially since he'd started thinking about the whole rat incident.

Robert looked at the bedspread, searching for any suspicious lumps. He'd become adept at spotting critters in his bed during his childhood, particularly after the escapade with his brother Lenny's pet snake. Running a flat palm over the bed, he sighed with relief when he found nothing suspicious.

Robert slowly walked around the room, looking behind curtains and under furniture for any other unseen visitors, but spotted nothing out of the ordinary. So Ruthie's call, while thoughtful, had apparently been unnecessary. It had also gotten him too keyed up and edgy to get back to work. Not because of any concerns about rats or towels or sheets, though.

She was downstairs in the kitchen. Right in the spot where they'd met, where everything had begun. "She does owe me some cheesecake," he mumbled thoughtfully.

And he was awfully hungry.

RUTHIE FINISHED writing a note for Friday's morning supervisor, then put away her notebook and paper. She tilted her head from side to side, feeling tense and edgy, obviously due to the stress of the evening, not to mention the week. It had been so hard talking to him, hearing his voice, knowing he was a mere three floors above her in his room.

He wanted her. That was still the most amazing re-

alization for Ruthie. His desire for her hadn't waned
after they'd made love. He wore it like a cloak, it shone
from his eyes, from his sexy grin. It came through his
voice in the most innocent of conversations. Ruthie
wasn't falsely modest, she knew she was an attractive
woman, in a small, bubbly, *fleshy* way. But she knew
she wasn't the type to induce the kind of passion that
made men crazy, persistent and relentless.

Until now. Until Robert. He truly desired her. And
his feelings were entirely reciprocated.

Pulling her hair free of the clip that held it at her
nape, she ran her fingers through its length. She
walked over to one of the large refrigerators, opening
the door to dig out a bottle of mineral water. She
needed something cold to drink to cool her off, especially after spending the past few moments thinking
about Robert. Simply hearing the man's voice through
a phone line got her hot and bothered.

Ruthie shut the refrigerator, opened the plastic bottle, and sipped from it. Shrugging her shoulders to
loosen them, she rubbed the tense muscles of her neck
with her fingers. Though it was midnight, she looked
forward to going home and relaxing in a hot tub before
bed.

When someone else's hand moved over hers, contin-
uing the massage, she closed her eyes and took a deep
breath. She knew who stood behind her. The stress
she'd been feeling changed, sparked with a new kind
of tension she recognized instantly. It was drugging,
intoxicating, purely sensual. "Robert?"

"Mm-hm," he murmured. He moved closer, using
both hands to knead the tight muscles of her shoulders
and upper arms. Ruthie let her head fall back, nearly
purring with pleasure.

"Long day?"

She nodded. "Why did you come here?" she asked dreamily, not even opening her eyes.

"You owe me some cheesecake. I'm hungry."

She felt his breath on the side of her face and knew if she leaned back a scant inch, she'd fall into him, their bodies would touch from cheek to hip.

She leaned. He groaned. Then he slid his arm across the front of her, from shoulder to shoulder, holding her tight as he began to press kisses to her temple, her cheekbone, and the line of her jaw.

She didn't move, didn't turn in his arms to face him. It was too delicious like this, facing away from him, standing frozen while he kissed a path down the heated flesh of her neck. His hand had free access to stroke her. When he moved his other arm to encircle her waist, pressing his palm flat against her belly to pull her tighter against himself, her legs went weak.

"No song and dance this time, Ruthie? No 'I want you—don't touch me'?"

She shook her head lethargically and leaned farther into him. "If you stop touching me I think I'll die."

Ruthie finally opened her eyes, and found herself staring at their merged shadows on the stainless steel refrigerator, unable to distinguish where her body ended and his began. She looked down, noting the size of his warm hands, pressed so possessively against her body—holding, not moving. She wanted him to touch her more thoroughly. More intimately. She shifted restlessly and was rewarded when he moved one hand lower, brushing past her breast in a light, heart-stopping caress.

She whimpered. Feeling dizzy, Ruthie reached out to place her hands flat against the door of the refrigerator. It was slick, hard. All her senses felt fully alive and Ruthie savored the different textures. The cool metal. His hot mouth. Her own racing heartbeat not quite drowning out the sound of his shallow breaths.

"Please," she said, not knowing exactly what she asked for.

He knew. He slid one hand into the neckline of her pale blue blouse, cupping her breast through her bra and stroking a lazy circle over her puckered nipple with his thumb. Ruthie bit her lip. Not finished, he moved his other hand lower, gliding across the front of her loose khaki skirt, then reaching her sex. He cupped her and she nearly flew apart in his arms.

"You make me crazy," he said with a groan.

Ruthie was completely beyond caring about anything but the pleasure he was making her feel with his lips, and oh, sweet heaven, his fingers. Everything that was between them seemed to disappear. She was ready to charge full steam ahead, damn the consequences, damn everything else.

Then the light came on.

"Anyone seen a big white rat in here?"

9

ROBERT THOUGHT he was going to blow up. He truly thought he was going to explode into a million pieces of energized, sexually frustrated flesh when the light came on.

He jerked away from Ruthie, reacting instinctively to protect her reputation. She tried to twist away, too, and between them they managed to get his hand stuck in her blouse. He muttered a curse. Meanwhile, Ruthie's blond-haired cousin Chuck strolled around the corner of some waist-high cabinets looking as bland and innocent as a child. "Ruthie?"

Robert felt like a kid caught with his hand in the cookie jar. Literally.

Ruthie groaned, then jerked backward, and Robert heard a funny little ripping sound as a button gave way. But at least his hand was free. He took a quick step away from her.

"Uh, yes, Chuck?" she said, her reddened face making a lie of her nonchalant tone.

Chuck looked back and forth between them, eyes narrowed suspiciously. "What's goin' on?"

"Nothing at all," Robert explained smoothly. "I was simply trying to help your cousin with something." He hoped the other man would have the sense to graciously leave it at that.

"Help her with what?"

"He was trying to help me find something," Ruthie hissed.

Oh, yeah, Robert had definitely been trying to help her find something. And judging by the way she'd been whimpering and squirming against him about sixty seconds before, he'd have to say she'd been pretty darn close to finding it. The thought of her incredible responsiveness made him ache and he mentally cursed the blond annoyance who'd interrupted them.

"What is the problem, Chuck?" Ruthie asked as she crossed her arms in front of her chest, obviously trying to cover up the fact that a button was missing. Robert quickly looked around and spotted it, small, silver, shiny, near one of the massive dishwashers a few feet away.

"I'm looking for Tina's pet," Chuck replied after casting another suspicious glance at them. "She can't find Max."

Ruthie groaned. "You're not serious."

"Why don't you come with me to look for him, Ruthie?"

Robert saw the look of dislike the young man sent in his direction, and suddenly suspected the innocent interruption had been completely intentional.

"I have to get out of here," Ruthie muttered. "I'm going home. You can spend the entire night finding that creature, but I'd better hear he's been caught by tomorrow morning, or I'm calling one of those guys with the mouse ears on his car!"

Robert almost laughed at the look of horror on the young man's face.

"That's cold, Ruthie!"

"Go look, Chuck."

He didn't budge. "I'll walk you to your car. It's late."

Robert wasn't about to let her run away again, at least not until they'd had a chance to talk, or... whatever. "I'll walk her out."

She looked back and forth between them, and Robert saw the indecision on her lovely face. She wanted him. There was no question that she wanted him. He saw it in her green eyes, in the way she held her arms tightly around her body, as if for strength. She leaned against the refrigerator, her legs probably still shaky. If they were alone he imagined he could take one step toward her and she'd be back in his arms, right where she belonged.

And she knew it too. So she obviously wasn't taking any chances. "All right, Chuck, give me a minute to get my things and you can walk me out."

"Ruthie, wait," Robert urged.

"Thank you for stopping by to talk about the hotel, Mr. Kendall," she said, obviously trying to pretend nothing was going on between them.

Robert wondered if she truly believed her cousin hadn't known exactly what he was interrupting. "Let me take you home."

"Ruthie's got a car," Chuck said, sounding exasperated.

"Don't you have a rat to find?"

"I think I found one," Chuck muttered, looking very much like a sullen kid.

Robert now knew for sure Ruthie's cousin had intentionally walked in on them. And, given the obstinate expression on the young man's face, he knew Chuck was not going to give Robert another minute alone with Ruthie.

"Tomorrow, Ruthie," Robert insisted as he watched her grab her purse and notebook. "I have to drive down to Baltimore for the day. Say you'll meet me tomorrow night when I get back." Chuck looked like he wanted to object, but Robert's challenging frown stopped him.

Ruthie looked around nervously, not meeting his eye. "I, uh...I don't know if that's possible. Friday nights are pretty busy around here. And I don't know that it's a good idea for us to...uh...meet again."

"That old song and dance?" he asked, shaking his head in disappointment. She was doing it once more. *I want you. Don't touch me.*

She obviously knew what he was thinking. Her cheeks grew pink, and she stood taller, squaring her shoulders. "No, not that. But the next time I decide to *dance* with you, I want it to be with a clear head. Let's think about our next meeting, make sure we're both in the right frame of mind to...dance, rather than acting on the spur of the moment when we happen to bump into each other."

He understood what she meant. She needed room, room to decide whether she wanted to go any further with their relationship. And she wanted to be alone, with a clear head, when she made that decision. With no heated caresses in a darkened kitchen to influence her. *So be it.*

"All right," he said with a single nod. "Call me in my room tomorrow night when you're finished work."

"You two were dancing?" Chuck asked, confusion evident on his handsome young face. "I thought you were kissing...."

Ruthie let out a giggle that completely eased the tension in the room. "Good night, Robert."

They shared an amused smile before Chuck took Ruthie's arm and led her out of the kitchen like a protective watchdog. That shared moment of humor lifted Robert's spirits tremendously. Okay, so she'd walked away from him. Again. But this time he knew she wasn't trying to walk away for good. She was backing off, giving them both time, planning their next meeting instead of just falling into it. He had to hope that meant she'd opened her eyes. And maybe her heart.

With a much lighter step than he'd had all day, Robert went upstairs to his room to go to bed. He took a quick look around as he entered, prepared for more terrorist acts, and wondered if he'd have to remake the bed again tonight. When he tugged back the bedspread, he realized he wouldn't.

Because it appeared he had no sheets at all.

THE QUESTION OF HOW Monica was reacting to the staff's sabotage was answered early the next morning. Robert had just finished shaving, shortly after eight, when the phone rang. He quickly answered, wondering if the office in Baltimore was calling to reschedule his appointment.

"They flooded my room!"

"Monica?"

She sounded furious. "Two imbeciles who look like rejects from the College for Stupid People came into my room, saying they had to check a problem with the pipes. And they flooded it! There's water gushing all over the bathroom as we speak. Then they left, saying they had to go get more tools."

Robert shook his head, glad she wasn't around to see the smile tugging his lips wide.

"This is the last straw, Robert! Yesterday, it took four phone calls and three hours to get my dinner brought up. Then, when I was getting ready for bed, I found a note from the maid saying she'd dropped my tooth-brush into the *toilet!*"

Somehow Robert contained the laugh that threat-ened to erupt from his lips. "Did you find the note be-fore or after you'd used the toothbrush?"

Monica muttered something that sounded like "I bet she *intentionally* left the note behind my makeup bag."

He grimaced. *After.*

"Look, Monica, obviously the Kerrigan is not up to your standards. There's nothing for you to do here. Why don't you just go back to New York?"

He was grasping at straws, never figuring she'd ac-tually listen to him. But she almost sounded relieved when she replied. "You're sure you can handle the rest of the negotiations without me?"

"Absolutely," he insisted, trying not to let her hear the relief in his voice. Monica's departure could only *help* negotiations!

"Fine. I'm leaving on the first flight I can get. I think there's one back to LaGuardia at eleven. Hopefully I'll have time to pack and go once these morons come back and fix the bathroom so I can take a shower."

Anxious to have her gone, Robert said, "Look, I'm leaving my room in half an hour anyway. I have a meeting down in Baltimore and I need to get on the road. You're welcome to come take a shower here." There was no way he would have made the offer if he hadn't been planning to leave his room, of course, but this seemed like an ideal way to get her out of Phila-delphia even faster.

"All right. I'll get some things together and be there in a few minutes."

After she hung up, Robert went back to the bath-room to finish getting shaved and dressed. He moved quickly, wanting to be walking out the door as Monica came in. He did, however, pause for a few moments before brushing his teeth. He scanned the counters, looking behind his shaving kit and even on the floor. "No note."

Reaching for his toothbrush, he looked at it closely, then tossed the thing in the trash can. He took a swig of mouthwash, and swished it around his mouth. He'd grab a new toothbrush in the sundry store downstairs on his way out of the hotel.

"Better safe than sorry."

RUTHIE WOKE UP Friday morning feeling much more energized and refreshed than anyone should after getting only five hours sleep. She'd thought she'd go home and toss and turn all night, mulling over what to do about her relationship with Robert. But she hadn't. She'd been out like a light as soon as her head hit the pillow.

She'd dreamed. Oh, yes, she'd dreamed. Her dreams had been eerily similar to what she recalled of Sunday night. But she imagined dreams couldn't compare to the reality. She only wished she could remember all the details.

Needing to speak with her uncle Henry about what she'd learned the night before, Ruthie quickly dressed and decided to head over to the hotel to speak with him in person. Though it was only eight o'clock she knew her uncle would already be in his office. When she got to the hotel, she made her way there and quickly told him about the staff's sabotage.

Henry was, of course, appalled. "Do you know who's responsible? Who thought up this scheme?"

Ruthie didn't. She assumed Tina had a hand in it, but

certainly couldn't lay the blame for everything at her door.

"I don't suppose it matters whose idea it was, Uncle Henry," Ruthie said, "as long as they all stop."

Her uncle looked out the window of his office, and Ruthie noted the way the early-morning sun caught the gray strands in his thinning blond hair. Her father would probably have looked very much like him. The thought brought a sharp pang of sadness, and she had to clench her fists.

"Well, I suppose this goes a long way in explaining the flood in Miss Winchester's room this morning."

Ruthie rolled her eyes and sighed. "Flood?"

As Henry explained what had happened that morning in Monica Winchester's room, Ruthie had to bite her lip to hold in a laugh. Her uncle painted such a vivid picture of the woman standing on a chair, shrieking at the two handymen as they left.

Ruthie knew she shouldn't take satisfaction in the other woman's difficult morning. But considering what Robert had told her about Monica Winchester—and the whole *condom* episode—she couldn't help thinking the brunette deserved what she got. She could tell by the slight smile on her uncle Henry's lips that he wasn't completely distraught by the incident, either.

After bidding her uncle a good day, Ruthie left his office, planning to return home. That was the plan. But her feet weren't in on it. They took her directly to the elevator.

She wanted to see Robert. He deserved to know that her uncle was going to make sure the staff toed the line. And she also thought she should inform him about what had happened to his colleague. *Sure, right, that's the only reason you're going to go up to his room at this time of morning,* a little inner voice said.

Ignoring it, Ruthie punched the elevator call button.

ROBERT WAS FULLY DRESSED and nearly ready to go by the time Monica came knocking on the door to his room. She'd arrived twenty minutes after her call, toiletry bag and clothing in tow. "Come on in," he said. "I was getting ready to leave."

"You're a darling, Robert," Monica said as she entered the room. She cast a quick look at his unmade bed, which very obviously had no sheets, and gave him a curious look.

"Don't ask."

Shrugging, Monica went into the bathroom and shut the door. Robert was putting the finishing touches on his tie and was about to reach for his suit jacket when a short knock sounded on the door. Figuring the maid was coming to see how he'd enjoyed his uncomfortable night sleeping on top of the covers, Robert yanked the door open. He blinked. "Ruthie?"

She greeted him with a bright smile. "I wanted to let you know, I talked to my uncle Henry this morning. You won't be having any more problems with the staff."

"Thank you," he said, still not quite believing she'd shown up. He wondered what it meant, her coming to see him first thing in the morning like this. Had she thought about what she wanted last night? Did this mean she was through putting up roadblocks? "I appreciate you coming to tell me in person."

"You're getting ready to go to Baltimore?"

He nodded. "Uh, yeah, I need to meet with some of the execs at our location there. I wish I weren't. I'd love to take you to breakfast." Mundane. Simple small talk that hid the real questions and answers burning in his brain. Did she want him? Was she ready to admit it? Was she going to give them a chance?

He was about to ask her. The words were coming off his tongue, when the bathroom door opened and Monica stepped out, wearing nothing but a white terry-cloth towel. "Robert, don't you have any soap in this room?"

His jaw dropped. The blood fell out of his face in one solid, heated rush. And for the first time in as long as he could remember, Robert couldn't come up with a word to say. He watched, struck mute, as Ruthie looked back and forth, from him, to the messy unmade bed, to Monica standing in the doorway. She stared at him, watching as he worked his mouth, choking out a few words, sounding like the idiot blubbering male of comic books and movies, caught in the act and trying to come up with lame excuses. "Ruthie, I..."

"I see it's not a good time for us to talk," she said quietly. Too quietly. This did not bode well.

"Wait, it's not—"

She didn't listen. Turning on her heel, she walked away, down the carpeted corridor toward the elevator. Robert stepped out of the room after her and nearly tripped over a heavily laden maid's cart, which was parked right outside his door. He tried to shove it out of the way. He succeeded only in getting himself wet as a bottle of disinfectant fell off the cart and squirted a long stream of pine-smelling fluid onto his pants leg. And on the floor. That earned him a glare from a maid, who'd chosen that moment to step out of a nearby room.

"Hold it right there, Ruthie," Robert ordered as he

tried to get around the cart and the maid, who was watching the unfolding scene with speculation in her eyes.

Ruthie didn't pause. As he hurried to catch up to her, he saw her shoulders shaking, and noted that her head was slumped forward. Crying? Was she crying? God, had he hurt her, even without being guilty of anything?

He grabbed her arm and spun her around, prepared to beg her to listen while he explained, apologized, anything! But instead of tears he saw... "Laughing? You're laughing?"

She nodded, holding her fingers against her lips as she tried to contain the giggles. She was unsuccessful, and laughter erupted from her mouth. "Oh, Robert, your face, you should have seen your face."

Feeling like he was in the middle of an episode of *The Twilight Zone*, he could only stare at her. "What are you talking about?"

She snorted another laugh. "Oh, my gosh, that's the first time I've seen you completely lost for words. Caught. *Busted.*" She laughed again, this time so hard that tears came to her eyes. "You looked like a deer facing down headlights."

Robert nearly sighed his relief. "I thought I was toast. You're not mad."

"About what? Your condom-killing co-worker using your shower because a couple of plumbing school flunkees decided to flood her room?"

She knew. She understood without being told why Monica had been in his room. And Robert realized something else. *She'd never doubted him.* The realization shocked him and gave Robert such a sudden rush of pleasure he could only smile.

He stared down at her, captivated by the energy in her sparkling green eyes, and knew he could be honest with her. "I did invite her to my room. But I would never have let her come if she hadn't said she was going to leave town as soon as she could get ready. I wanted her gone."

"Why?"

He cupped her chin in his hand, his fingers caressing the soft skin of her temple and tangling in the fine strands of hair there. "So I can have some time to figure out what the hell to do about this whole mess."

She tugged away. "What's happening between us is a mess?"

"I meant everything. I want to do the right thing, Ruthie. For you. For me. For your family. I'm going to make this work out."

He saw her eyes widen with happiness and knew he'd made the right choice. He'd thought about it long and hard the night before, and though he'd lit upon no solution, he'd acknowledged that he couldn't help his boss force the Sinclairs out into the street. There had to be something he could do to keep the Sinclair family involved in the Kerrigan after Winchester Hotels took it over.

The sudden joy in her eyes reaffirmed his decision. She leaned up and pressed a sweet kiss on his cheek. "I knew I could trust you. About everything," she said.

"So, if you knew why Monica was in my room, why did you walk away so fast?"

She raised an eyebrow. "I had no intention of having any kind of private conversation with you in front of witnesses. Especially not condom-murderers who try to trap men."

"I'm sure she didn't do that," he protested with a

shaky laugh. "And what did you want to talk to me about?"

Hearing a noise behind him, Robert turned around and saw a man exit another room. He gave them a curious stare as he waited for the elevator. A few feet beyond him, the wide-eyed maid continued to watch them, pretending she was busy refolding towels that had fallen off her cart during Robert's wrestling match with it.

Ruthie also noticed the audience. Thinking quickly, she grabbed Robert's arm. "Come here," she said, leading him a few steps away to a door marked Housekeeping Only. Sending a quelling glance in the direction of Suze, the third-floor maid, Ruthie pushed the door open and tugged him into the closet. She reached for the switch and flipped on an overhead light.

"You're so romantic," he said, laughter in his voice as he looked around at the shelves laden with linens, towels, spare pillows and cleaning supplies. "Remind me to grab some of those sheets before we leave, wouldja?"

"Shut up and kiss me," Ruthie ordered, feeling strangely euphoric, happy, nearly giddy. Though she'd already decided to go full steam ahead and pursue the crazy, wild, wonderful feelings she had for Robert Kendall, now that he'd told her he wasn't going to proceed with taking over the Kerrigan, she felt even better about her decision.

"No song and dance this time, Ruthie?" he asked intently. She knew he was making sure she knew her own mind and the realization made her want him even more.

"I want you. *Please* touch me."

She didn't have to ask him twice, didn't even have

time to take a deep breath for courage. Suddenly his lips were on hers, hungry, sweet, both demanding and promising. She opened her mouth for him, inviting him deeper, welcoming his tongue with her own.

Before she realized what he was doing, Ruthie found herself being picked up. He had his hands around her waist, and he lifted her, bringing her shoulders level with his. Ruthie slipped her arms around his neck to hold him tightly as they continued to kiss, deeply, endlessly, with both passion that enthralled, and sweetness that warmed.

She wanted to cry when he moved his mouth away from hers, but sighed in satisfaction as he began to kiss the hot flesh of her neck. His thick, dark hair was damp beneath her fingers, his freshly shaven cheek smooth next to her own. Ruthie hooked one leg around his, rubbing her body restlessly against him, seeking relief, wanting his heat, wanting the thick, heavy erection she felt pressing against her pelvis. He groaned as she rubbed herself against him but Ruthie didn't stop, couldn't stop, needing some way to ease the incredible pressure building inside her.

He slowly lowered her to the floor, letting her stand on her own shaky legs. She had to lean back against a shelf to avoid falling to the cramped floor. "Plenty of linens, no place to lie down," he muttered.

Ruthie took a quick look around and realized he was right. The closet was only about four by four, crowded with shelves and supplies. "Standing room only."

She heard him chuckle as he noted the suggestive tone in her voice. Hot liquid lust shot through her, pooling between her thighs as mental pictures invaded her mind. Her dress tossed aside, her legs wrapped around his lean hips as he held her bottom in his big, warm hands. And Ruthie holding on for dear life, leaning back against the wall as he thrust into her.

"Aw, hell, Ruthie, I don't suppose you brought..."

Her fantasy evaporated and she nearly whimpered. "No. I wasn't exactly planning this for this morning. I kinda had this image of meeting you tonight in the kitchen again."

He groaned. "You know what I've been imagining?"

She shook her head, unable to speak as he continued to work his magic on her neck with his lips. She arched back, wanting him to go further, and he complied, sliding his tongue along the scooped neckline of her loose cotton dress.

"I've been remembering Sunday night." His voice was a husky, sensuous whisper, scraping along her sensitive nerve endings much as his tongue was scraping along the high curves of her breasts. "Picturing you on that high butcher-block worktable. Leaning back, your thighs open for me, wearing nothing but those white stockings."

"Oh, my," she moaned, feeling weaker, hotter, wetter. "And where are you in this fantasy? Standing between my legs?" *Thrusting wildly? Holding my hips tightly and driving yourself into me while I strain up to meet you?*

"Not at first." He reached behind her back and very slowly dragged the zipper of her dress down, then nudged one sleeve off her shoulder. Ruthie let it fall, tilting to help it along, wanting him to continue using his mouth to kiss her, suckle her, murmur his fantasies against her heated flesh.

"Not standing," he said on a warm breath, his sultry whisper doing crazy things to her senses. "Sitting. On the stool at your feet. Admiring how beautiful you are.

Looking my fill. Touching you. Tasting you, every bit of you. Using my mouth to memorize the textures and flavors of you until you scream and explode like you did Sunday night."

"Oh, Robert," she managed to say between heaving breaths. His fantasy filled her mind, the image of his dark head between her pale legs nearly made Ruthie explode right then.

"Then, only then, standing and sliding into you until I explode, too."

If the closet hadn't been so small, so packed with shelves, Ruthie might have fallen into a limp, wet puddle right there.

Robert must have sensed her weakness, because he held her tightly around the hips as he continued his slow exploration of the curves of her breasts. He tugged the remaining sleeve off her shoulder and pulled the dress down, letting it fall to the floor at their feet.

"Robert, we don't have any..."

"Shhh, it doesn't matter. There are so many other delightful things we can do," he whispered as he undid the clasp of her bra, stepping back to watch as her breasts fell free. His eyes darkened in appreciation, and Ruthie stood confidently before him. "You're so beautiful, Ruthie."

Now, wearing only a pair of yellow bikini panties and her brown leather sandals, Ruthie waited for whatever *delight* was coming next. When he leaned over to catch the tip of her breast and suck it deeply into his mouth, she arched forward and wound her hands in his hair.

As much as she wanted him to, he didn't linger, merely pressing sweet wet kisses, tiny love bites on one breast, before shifting to pay attention to the other. Her nipples were hard, pebbled, and as he caught one in his mouth and swirled his tongue over it, Ruthie closed her eyes and gave in to the sensations coursing through her body.

Then he knelt down before her, running his mouth down her stomach, kissing her belly and taking a deep breath as if imprinting her scent on his brain. She looked down, saw the dark hair next to her white skin, knew what he was doing, went liquid and willing, needing his touch, his most intimate kiss.

He slid his hand up her leg, stroking the quivering muscles there, then touching the elastic leg band of her panties. She parted her legs slightly, giving him access, and heard his breath catch as he watched. Then he slipped a finger beneath the nylon fabric, tugging it free of the moisture slickening her aroused flesh.

When he tested that moisture, sliding his finger into the sensitive folds of her skin, Ruthie had to grab his shoulders for support. Then he was pulling the fabric away, tugging her panties off and tossing them aside. His lips replaced his fingertip as he kissed her—so deeply, so intimately—with an intensity that felt so damn good it nearly hurt. He used his tongue and teeth to find her throbbing center of sensation, then played with it until Ruthie's sighs turned into whimpers. When he moved his hand back and slid his finger deep inside her body, matching the rhythm he'd already set with his tongue, her whimpers became moans.

And when she reached the precipice, when he brought her to that white-hot explosion of delicious warmth, and sparks shot all around her body in an instant of ultimate pleasure, her wavering moans turned into a weak, high-pitched scream.

ROBERT WATCHED HER for several moments, knowing he could remain kneeling at her feet looking up at her beautiful face for hours. Her skin was flooded with color, her lips open and her breath coming in short choppy pants. Maybe a housekeeper's closet had never been high on his list of erotic locales, but after this, Robert had a feeling it was going to remain one of his favorite places. He imagined he'd forever associate the clean scents of pine and lemon with the heady, musky flavor of Ruthie's desire.

Pressing one more kiss into the silky red curls between her thighs, Robert slowly stood, watching her, waiting for her eyes to open so he could see the limpid pleasure shining from them.

When a sharp knock sounded on the door of the closet, her eyes opened all right. But not in lethargic ecstasy. Nope, he reckoned he'd have to call it panic.

"Housekeeping," a muffled voice called from the other side of the door.

"Oh, no," Ruthie said frantically. He watched her gaze dart from the tightly closed door, to Robert, down to her own completely naked—completely luscious— body.

"I locked the door," he said with a gentle smile.

She stared at him like he was simpleminded. "She has a key, ya know!"

Wincing, Robert quickly bent over and grabbed Ruthie's dress from the floor. He almost didn't spot her white bra, which lay limply on a pile of starched sheets. Robert watched as she retrieved it and tried to yank it on without flipping it around to do up the hooks from the front first. Impossible, given Ruthie's more than generous assets! Holding back a chuckle, he gently turned her around and fastened the hooks himself, then stepped back as she tugged the dress down to cover herself.

The knock came again. "Ruthie? It's Suze!"

Seeing that she was properly covered, Robert gave a sigh of regret that their delicious little interlude was about to end. He unlocked the door and opened it. The maid he'd bumped into earlier, when rushing after Ruthie, stuck her head in the closet, giving them a big grin that showed off one gold front tooth. "Just thought ya might wanna know she's gone."

"Who?" Ruthie asked, still looking dazed and out of sorts.

"The brunette. She left about five minutes ago, once I told her they'd gotten her room fixed and cleaned up. She seemed to think you'd left town for a meeting," she said, looking directly at Robert. He knew the woman hadn't told Monica where he'd really gone, and gave her a smile of thanks.

"So, if you want to be alone to...talk...you don't have to stay here in the closet. And, uh, I've made your bed." The woman didn't offer any apologies. Right now, Robert didn't care in the least.

"I've grown rather fond of this closet," Robert said, giving Ruthie a sly grin.

She smiled weakly, still trying to appear nonchalant, as if all they'd been doing in the linen closet was having a private—very private—conversation.

"I'll see if the coast is clear," Suze said with a wink, ducking back out of the closet. Robert watched her go, then caught sight of something behind Ruthie's back. Hoping the maid hadn't seen what he was seeing, Rob-

ert had to bend over, coughing, to try to disguise a
burst of laughter.

Ruthie's tiny yellow nylon underwear hung limply
like a flag of surrender from the wooden handle of an
old mop.

10

WHEN SUZE TOLD them the hallway was completely empty, Robert tugged Ruthie out of the housekeeping closet toward his room. He'd tucked her underwear into his pocket without letting her see, which wasn't hard since she'd kept her head down, avoiding meeting Suze's eyes. Or his own.

He was half afraid she'd be too embarrassed to ever look at him again. But when they got into his room, and he shut the door firmly behind them, she literally threw her arms around his neck and kissed him hard on the mouth.

"What was that for?" he asked with a soft laugh when she pulled away, her eyes bright and shining with pleasure and a wide smile on her lips.

"I just wanted to kiss you in the broad daylight," she said, gesturing toward the window letting in the bright rays of early morning sun.

"I've been wanting to do the same thing since the night we met," he admitted. "Though you wear moonlight very well, I've wanted to see the sun picking up the gold in your hair."

She walked across the room toward the window then reached behind her neck to undo a large clasp holding her hair back. "Like this?" she asked as she let it fall free.

"Not exactly," he said as he walked across the room

toward her. When he reached her side, he slid his hands into the curls at her neck. "I want to see it spread over the white pillowcase on my bed."

His voice was low, heated. Ruthie's eyes darkened as Robert began to undo the tie he'd put on a half hour earlier. A half hour? Seemed impossible that their relationship could have changed, intensified so dramatically, in as small a time frame as thirty minutes. Bringing Ruthie to her peak of sexual satisfaction had given Robert the most incredible sense of accomplishment. And had given him such sensual pleasure as well. He could still taste her on his lips and tongue, still feel the softness of her thigh against his cheek.

The memory brought a sense of urgency to his hands as he unfastened the buttons of his dress shirt. Ruthie watched, her lips parted, her eyes wide, as he tugged the shirt free of his trousers, leaving it hanging loosely on his shoulders.

"Let me," she murmured, brushing his hands away. Ruthie couldn't just be a spectator, as delightful as it was to watch him undress. She needed to touch. Needed to make him feel some of the ecstasy he'd given her moments before.

She was still reeling over that. She'd completely lost control, lost inhibition, reveled in the feelings he'd brought forth in her body. She hadn't known she was capable of it until he'd shown her she was.

She undressed him slowly, biting her lip in a vain attempt to control her heavy breathing. "I feel like a kid on Christmas," she said with a sigh. "I was always a very slow unwrapper, I picked off every bit of tape and never tore the paper so the morning would last a long time."

"And when you finished unwrapping, did you play

with all your toys at once, or zone in on one that was your favorite?" he asked, his voice both light with humor and thick with innuendo.

She looked up at him, curling her lips into a sultry smile. "When I had a new toy I was particularly fond of, I played with it for days."

"I think I'm in trouble," he replied thickly.

"I know you're in trouble."

After Ruthie unfastened his trousers, she slipped her hands into the waistband and pushed them down. Slowly. Unwrapping. He had such a beautiful body— long and lean, rippled with muscle and shaped to fit her hands.

She loved looking at him, truly looking, not sneaking embarrassed peeks, nor watching through a cloudy haze of champagne. When he stepped back to kick off his shoes and socks and push his trousers to the floor, she watched, liking the play of sunlight on his skin, the rich dark shade of his hair.

Now clad only in a pair of tightly fitted white boxers that barely contained his erection, Robert moved closer, reaching around her neck to unzip her dress. She let it fall away, then stepped free of it. "Oh, my goodness," Ruthie said with a chuckle as she felt the slight morning chill touch her body. "I think I forgot something."

"I've got them," he said as he nuzzled her neck and reached around to unclasp her bra. "Not that I'm offering to give them back, mind you."

"No? A trophy?"

"Maybe."

Ruthie chuckled, remembering an old movie that had been one of her favorites as a teenager. "As long as you don't sell glimpses of them for a dollar a pop."

The laughter died from her lips as he got serious, catching her mouth in a hot, wet kiss. Ruthie shivered in his arms, savoring the texture and sweet taste of his tongue. She rubbed against him, delighting in the ticklish sensation of his dark wiry chest hair against her nipples. A low, pleased moan rose out of her throat as Robert caught her breasts with his fingers, stroking them, plucking them to taut peaks.

Wanting even more, Ruthie slipped her hands into the waistband of his boxers and carefully worked them down. Intentionally brushing the back of one hand against his erection, she sighed with satisfaction as his muscles tightened and he hissed his pleasure against her lips.

She grew bolder. Pushing the last of his clothes to the floor, she waited while he kicked them away, then moved her hands back, cupping him, testing his breadth. Ruthie marveled at the warmth of his flesh in her palms and loved that she brought forth such a powerful need in him. Becoming more frantic, she backed up, pulling him with her until they both fell on the bed. "You do have..."

"Yes," he muttered before lowering his lips to kiss a path down her throat, across her chest until he finally sucked one pert nipple deeply into his mouth.

She felt the pull of his lips throughout her body, not just on her breast, and the ache between her thighs intensified. Twisting anxiously against him, Ruthie silently demanded more, knowing they could communicate like longtime lovers, without words, merely with sighs, touches and intimate caresses.

Obviously understanding her need, Robert rolled over and grabbed an unopened box of condoms out of a bedside table drawer. Ruthie nodded, urged him to go faster, unable to stand the thought of not having him inside her for another minute.

And then he was. Sheathed and inside her. Deep. Not moving for a moment. Just touching her in a place no one ever had before. It was beyond physical, somehow, but also brought to Ruthie the most unbelievably delicious sense of fullness.

She closed her eyes, squeezing him deep inside, wondering how she'd ever survived the first twenty-eight-and-a-half years of her life without ever feeling this complete.

"It wasn't a dream," she whispered on a sigh.

"It's better than a dream, love," Robert said as he pressed a sweet kiss to her mouth.

She opened her eyes, looking up at the face of this man she'd known for mere days. The man who had imprinted himself on her brain, her body, and now, she suspected, her heart.

"Don't let it end," she whispered as she wrapped her legs around his thighs and her arms around his shoulders. She pressed tightly against him so it felt as if they were one person, caught up in the deliciousness of sensation and the powerful swell of emotion inside her. She wished she could feel this perfect forever. "Please don't let it end, Robert."

As he moved within her, slowly, languorously, building up the fire he'd started in her nearly a week before, he said, "It's never gonna end, Ruthie."

His words, offered in the heartbeat between one deep kiss and another, meant more to her than he'd probably ever intended. And when he took her higher and higher, when their bodies demanded more and they thrust against each other with powerful need and they both grew slick and damp with exertion and pleasure, she realized she almost believed him.

ROBERT MISSED HIS MEETING. He did, at least, muster up the energy to place a call to the Baltimore office and tell them he wasn't coming. He offered no explanation. And didn't care a bit that for the first time in as long as he could remember, he was completely blowing off his responsibilities.

"Are you hungry?" he asked Ruthie, glancing at the clock and noting it was well past noon.

She snuggled against him in the bed, tucking her body against his. "I have to say I've worked up an appetite this morning," she said with a yawn.

Oh, yeah. He'd worked up an appetite, too. And she'd helped him satisfy it. Twice already. He had a feeling they weren't finished snacking yet, though. It took nothing more than a darkening of her eyes or the brush of her hand on his face and he wanted her all over again.

"So, should we call for room service?"

She pulled away and looked up at him. "We can go downstairs to the restaurant."

"Are you sure, Ruthie? I do understand if you don't want to make us too...public yet. At least as far as your family goes. And the staff. I assume they'll all think you're fraternizing with the enemy."

"Fraternizing? Is that what you call it? Sheesh, and here I thought it was called delicious, body-rocking lovemaking."

He laughed out loud and tugged her tighter against his side, liking how she curled up against him and slipped one bare leg over his. "We could just order a pizza."

"For breakfast?"

"Ruthie, it's nearly one o'clock. You fell asleep."

She moved her hand across his chest in a light caress, then slipped it lower, teasingly playing with the sparse hair on his belly. "Did I?" she said softly. "Sleeping. Hm, I have to ask, Robert, what is it about being in your company that makes me have these amazingly erotic, kinky dreams?"

That got his attention. "Kinky?"

"Maybe just a little kinky," she said, a sultry tone in her voice as she leaned forward to press a heated kiss on his chest.

IT WAS NEARLY THREE when they finally left the room in search of food. Ruthie wondered, as they entered the elevator, how she could possibly walk through the hotel lobby, within sight of friends, family, and co-workers, and not show the world exactly what she'd been doing for the past several hours.

Making love with a stranger. No, not a stranger anymore. She hadn't known him long, but on a deep, internal level, Ruthie felt she knew Robert Kendall very, very well. Physically, she knew him better than she'd ever known another person in her life. But it went deeper, beyond the physical.

They hadn't only made love. In the morning hours in his room, they'd laughed together, talked and whispered, touched and sighed. He'd told her about his family, his upbringing. He'd made her see his childhood when he'd talked about his brothers; he had such a powerful way of describing things, making them real and vivid. She could visualize the first time he'd had to change a diaper, as a boy of six, wearing a surgical mask from a play doctor's kit, his father's goggles, and his mother's bright yellow, rubber dishwashing gloves. She'd giggled as he mentioned his hands had fallen asleep because he'd secured the gloves at the elbows with rubber bands to be sure nothing from the diaper actually touched his skin.

He told her about living in New York, painting word pictures that made her want to see it with him, to experience the city's art and culture and restaurants by his side.

They found they did have things in common. Maybe not books, or music, or movies. But on a deeper level. They shared a belief in the goodness of people. That was a pleasant surprise to Ruthie, who had gotten used to being told she was too trusting. Their political views also meshed, as did the sense of humor that had attracted them to each other from the very beginning.

And they shared joy. She loved his smile and he adored her dimples and that was all that seemed to matter to either of them during those sunny morning hours.

Ruthie didn't know if she'd ever experienced such a magical day. She wondered if she ever would again.

"Okay?" he asked, sliding his arm around her waist as she looked up to watch the numbers above the elevator door.

"Fine," she said with a smile. "Though I don't suppose I would be feeling so confident if you hadn't given me my underwear back!"

His eyes widened and he threw back his head to laugh, the sound booming in the small, confined elevator. He caught her hand in his and squeezed it tight. "I let you *borrow* them only because you reminded me of how strong those gusts of wind can be in the lobby when the front doors are opened."

She raised an eyebrow. "Wouldn't want to give any blue-haired old ladies a heart attack at the check-in desk."

They were still holding hands when the door to the elevator slid open. Ruthie looked out and saw Chuck standing outside.

"Hiya, Ruthie," her cousin said with a grin. He looked back and forth between Ruthie and Robert. "Whatcha been up to? Haven't seen you around today."

"Oh, nothing much," Ruthie lied, feeling her cheeks go hot. Maybe he wouldn't notice. After all, this *was* Chuck.

"Your face is so red—you're such a bad fibber, Ruthie. Anyway, you're here now, so I guess I'm outta the pool."

Ruthie raised a questioning brow as she and Robert exited the elevator. Chuck did not enter it, though he'd obviously been waiting right outside the door.

"What pool, Chuck?" she prompted, wondering if her cousin had gotten into trouble again for practicing his surf maneuvers in the hotel pool. The last time he'd cracked his head open and had to be taken to the emergency room for stitches.

"The betting pool. Me, Celly, Tina and Suze have been placing bets on what time you'd finally show up down here."

Ruthie heard Robert snicker and she shot him a glare. "I can't imagine what you're talking about."

"I was way off," Chuck said with a rueful shrug. "I figured you'd hide out til after dark, call in sick, then sneak down the back stairs. Knowing how embarrassed you get, I figured you'd never come down here in broad daylight."

Ruthie began to fear she understood what he was talking about. "Are you telling me everyone has been talking about...about..."

"Well, geez, Ruthie, Suze has the biggest mouth in Philadelphia."

Ruthie swayed and was glad for the supportive hand Robert had pressed against the small of her back. "Suze..."

Chuck just nodded. "Well, gotta go."

He pushed the button for the elevator, which opened immediately. Chuck stepped inside, giving Ruthie a grin and offering Robert an obvious thumbs-up. "Hey, sorry about the whole revenge thing," he told Robert. "I was pretty ticked when I heard about what happened between you guys Sunday night."

"Oh, good grief, everyone knows about that, too?" Ruthie wailed.

"Nah, I didn't tell anybody that part. I heard you and Celly talking about it."

He *had* heard them. "And you were part of this sabotage effort going on against Robert?"

"I kinda started it," Chuck said. "But that was before."

"Before what?" Ruthie asked, not sure she wanted to know the answer.

"Before we all realized the guy was crazy about you," Chuck said as the door began to close.

Ruthie felt her face get even hotter as she wondered what on earth Robert must be thinking of her cousin's announcement.

As if things weren't bad enough, Chuck stuck his hand out to block the slowly closing doors of the elevator, and leaned out. "By the way, those housekeeping closet doors must be real thin. Geez, Ruthie, I sure never figured you for a screamer.''

Ruthie waited for the floor to open up and swallow her whole. And Robert just stood beside her laughing.

ROBERT HADN'T HAD a vacation in over three years. So when he called his New York office late Friday afternoon and informed his boss that he wanted to take some personal time, he got no argument. James Winchester had, of course, asked how things were going with the Kerrigan negotiations, and Robert had honestly told him he had some misgivings about the way the deal was playing out. He didn't want to get into specifics over the phone, but promised James he'd meet with him when he got back.

He had two weeks to put everything else aside, his job, the hotel, all the reasons he and Ruthie weren't compatible, and just be with her. Robert needed to explore the feelings she aroused in him, feelings he'd never experienced before. And they both needed to determine what these intense emotions they had toward each other meant. Not to mention where they might lead. Two weeks didn't seem nearly long enough.

They were inseparable the entire time. He kept his room at the hotel, though he never slept there, just to keep up appearances. He supposed it didn't make much difference. Everyone at the Kerrigan, from her uncle to kitchen workers, knew they were involved.

He stayed with her at her little apartment, sharing her smaller, four-poster bed, and really liking how the two of them fit in it together. He'd never been comfortable sleeping with anyone else—too many years of sharing a room with one or two brothers, he supposed—but found that since meeting Ruthie Sinclair, he couldn't sleep if she *wasn't* in his arms.

Ruthie took some time off, too. She obviously loved Philadelphia, its history and its colonial charm, and showed him what the city had to offer. He found himself caught up in her enthusiasm, as usual.

One night they found common ground at the movies, going to see a World War II love story. And Ruthie had been just fine right up until a major battle scene, when she'd hurried out of the theater with one hand over her mouth and another over her stomach. Thankful she'd spared his shoes, he figured he'd rent that one on video sometime to see how it ended.

They ate out a lot, and she cooked for him even more. They walked for hours, talked endlessly. And they made love so often Robert wondered how he could still want her so much. Somehow he didn't think that would ever change.

They sailed on a local lake one sunny spring afternoon, until Ruthie remembered that the reason she hadn't been on a boat in years was that she got seasick. By the time they got back to shore, her face was as green as the surface of the water. Ruthie had pushed past him to get out of the boat as quickly as possible, and had accidentally knocked him over the side and into the lake.

They met her great-aunts for breakfast one morning and Robert fell in love with both of them. Lila had been a hoot telling them stories about her days as a Mae West wannabe making really bad B movies in Hollywood. Flossie had been as sweet, charming and talkative as a little bird. Robert could hardly wait until his next birthday so she'd give him back the engraved pocket knife his father had given him in high school.

No matter where they went, what they did, Robert felt the same sense of joyful freedom he'd felt the night they met. Because of her. Because of that smile, those dimples. Her amazing green eyes lit up with that sparkle of joy. He liked that he put it there. No, he *loved* that he put it there.

He was falling in love with her. Falling, hell. He already *had* fallen in love with her. He'd loved her from the night they met, even though logic told him that wasn't possible.

He hadn't told her yet, sensing that Ruthie still hadn't quite worked out in her mind exactly what kind of long-term relationship they might have together. But he'd been thinking about it. For the first time in his life he was visualizing a future that involved someone else.

She'd love New York. And he'd love showing her the world.

"I hate to leave," he told her early Sunday morning, the day he was scheduled to fly home. "You're sure you can't take the week off and come with me?"

Ruthie was tempted. She would have loved to see the city through his eyes. Heck, she would have loved to see none of the city—just the inside of his apartment—if it meant they could have more time together. She curled up against him in the bed, sliding a bare leg over his and an arm across his waist. "Don't I wish. But, no, I've taken enough time off in the past few days. You're coming back soon, though, aren't you?"

"Absolutely. I wish I could come next weekend, but I just can't. But the following one, don't make any plans. Meet me back here, right in this spot, one week from Friday night."

"Almost two weeks," she said with a sigh. "I do

have to work that night, you know. Fridays are impossible. Maybe you could come to the hotel and meet me in the kitchen."

"Only if you wear..."

She looked up into his eyes and puckered her lips flirtatiously. "My white stockings?"

He grinned. "I was gonna say your butt-ugly green dress. But, if you insist..."

Ruthie's punishing little pinch on his ribs turned into a caress when he caught her smiling mouth in a warm good-morning kiss. Then she settled back onto his chest. "We escaped the rat debacle unscathed. I really don't think the Health Department would look kindly at the chef having torrid sex on the food preparation table."

"Okay," he said with a put-upon sigh. "I guess we'd better stick to your bedroom. But, could you maybe lose the battery out of your clock?" He glanced toward her black-cat clock and gave a mock shiver. "He makes me nervous. It's like he's always watching, then rolling his eyes in shocked disbelief."

Ruthie smirked. "I don't think there's much *left* for him to see that could shock him."

"We've been doing something shocking?"

She moaned, a sound of pleasure coming from deep in her throat, and stretched languorously against him, liking the way his body reacted instantly as her leg moved higher.

"I'd say your friend Bobby was pretty shocked," Robert said with an evil chuckle.

Ruthie pushed at his chest, and frowned at him, scolding, "Poor Bobby. He was horrified when you answered the door wearing my pink bathrobe."

"Hey, what was I supposed to do? You confiscated

my clothes and threw them in the laundry, then got in the shower and wouldn't let me join you."

"Well, you had already showered," she said with a sheepish grin. "After I got seasick in your general direction, then shoved you into a slimy, algae-covered pond. Remember?"

"Forgiven."

"You're not."

"For what?"

"For being so rude to Bobby. Poor thing came over to apologize, to tell me the reason he had been so dismayed by my proposition was because he'd thought I was an innocent virgin saving myself for my wedding night. Then he found you in my robe and me coming out of the bathroom in nothing but a towel!"

Robert smiled as he remembered the scene, and Ruthie gave him a little punch in the upper arm.

"Hey," he protested, "don't ask me to apologize for letting the guy know what a moron he was. If he cared for you so much that he was considering marriage, then, dammit, he should have said so and thanked you for offering him such a precious gift as yourself." He lowered his voice. "He wasn't nearly good enough for you, anyway."

Ruthie sucked in a breath, hearing the intensity in his voice. Feeling his muscles tighten against her hand, she caressed his neck, twining her fingers in his hair. "I never would have married him. I didn't love him. I wanted to be in love, but I knew I wasn't."

Maybe he heard something in her voice, some unspoken declaration. Suddenly he wasn't laughing anymore, he was staring at her with heart-stopping intensity. She wondered if he knew how soft and gentle his expression had become, how his eyes studied every inch of her face, as if he wanted the memory of her features to last his whole life. He looked at her with tenderness. With desire. With more?

If he looked deeply enough, she knew he would see the same emotions reflected back at him from her eyes. Yes, the desire. Yes, the tenderness. Yes, genuine liking and pleasure.

And oh, yes, there was so much more.

She loved him. She'd wanted him from the moment they met, and had loved him for nearly as long. If he looked hard enough, he would certainly see that. She didn't try to hide it.

She did not, however, voice her feelings. Because, deep down, somewhere in the tiny little pessimistic corner of herself that she seldom acknowledged, Ruthie questioned whether this was all real. Had the past few weeks happened, or had they been purely fantasy? Even if it had all happened, was he truly coming back to her? What would happen between them when he did?

So she stared at him. She touched him. She told him she loved him in as many ways as she could without ever saying a word. And when he kissed her goodbye that afternoon, her lips said, "See you soon," and her heart said, "I love you. Please come back to me."

11

"YOU LOOK LIKE HELL."

Ruthie shot Celeste a dirty look. "You can say that, after ten days lying on a beach sipping rum drinks served with little umbrellas."

A smile curved her cousin's lips upward and Ruthie watched as Celeste curled up like a cat on the sofa. Ruthie had been pleased to see Celeste, of course. In the week and a half since Robert had left, her sunny apartment had grown oppressively silent. This morning, however, she really wasn't feeling well and had still been lazing in bed when her cousin had knocked at ten.

She'd been depressed, tired and mopey ever since he'd gone. Partly because she missed him. Partly because she wondered if he'd really come back. Mostly because she had gotten used to his lazy grin in the mornings and his heated caresses at night.

"From what I hear around the hotel," Celeste said, giving Ruthie a piercing look, "it sounds like you out-did me again. Wasn't it bad enough you showed me up on my wedding night? Did you have to have more sex during my honeymoon than I did, too?"

Ruthie smiled at her cousin's disgruntled expression. "I'm sure that's an exaggeration. Dain doesn't look like the type to not take full advantage of his honeymoon."

"We were ten days late leaving, remember?"

"So?"

Her cousin tilted her head and raised an eyebrow. "So, *we* were late...but *I* wasn't."

Ruthie got the picture. "Poor Dain."

"Talk about lousy timing. Can you imagine having to try to ask a French-speaking Caribbean store clerk where to find the tampons? In front of a store full of people?"

Ruthie winced. "You must have been mortified."

"Me? Heck no, I was back in the hotel lying on a heating pad they managed to scrounge up for me. I'm talking about Dain! He sulked for hours. I'll probably never be able to get the man to pick up something like that again as long as I live."

At the thought of Celeste's tall, gorgeous new husband having to explain the intricacies of feminine products to someone who didn't speak his language, Ruthie laughed aloud for the first time in days.

"Tea?" Ruthie asked as she got up to make herself some.

"Sure. So, obviously you and this Mr. Kendall made up," Celeste said while Ruthie put the kettle on. "I guess this means you were more than *business?*"

"I guess it does," Ruthie said.

"So why are you looking so dumpy and down?"

"Gee, thanks for the compliment," Ruthie said as she returned to the living room to sit across from her cousin.

"You have dark circles under your eyes and you're pale."

"Just tired."

"Lovesick."

"That, too."

Celeste's eyes widened. "You're in love with him?"

Ruthie nodded. "Afraid so."

"Does he feel the same way?"

"I don't know," Ruthie said. "For all I know, I may never see him again."

Celeste stood and walked over to sit on the arm of Ruthie's chair. She brushed Ruthie's hair off her brow, then leaned down and gave her a quick, one-armed hug. "He's a good guy, Ruthie. Mom told me you said he was giving up this idea of taking over the Kerrigan, and he obviously did that because he has feelings for you. You'll see him again. And I'm sure he's called."

Ruthie nodded. "Every day."

"He's crazy about you," Celeste insisted.

She hoped Celeste was right. In her heart, Ruthie agreed with her cousin. She and Robert had never discussed the Kerrigan situation during the two weeks they'd spent together, each obviously walking on eggshells to avoid anything that could come between them. But she knew darn well the reason he'd backed off the deal was because of his relationship with her.

So, no, she couldn't believe Robert would just walk away.

But not seeing him again wasn't her only fear. "Even if he does come back, it's just buying time. There's obviously no future for us."

Her cousin looked truly surprised. "Why not?"

"He doesn't want any of the things I want, Celly. Family. Lots of kids. Being tied to one place and getting wrapped deeply in the roots of something...like the Kerrigan."

When the kettle whistled, Celeste told Ruthie to remain where she was, and went into the kitchen to make their tea. Ruthie appreciated the solicitous gesture. "Thank you," she said when Celeste returned, carefully carrying two cups.

"Now how can you know he doesn't want any of those things? Has he come right out and told you?"

"Yes."

Celeste looked surprised. "He has? Really?"

Ruthie nodded miserably. "To him, the Kerrigan's just a building, a family is a group of people you eat turkey with every November and the rest of the year love via Ma Bell. And he had all the child-rearing he ever wanted helping to raise his brothers as a kid."

"Wow, Ruthie, I'm sorry," Celeste said, not making any effort to give her false hope or cheer her up.

Ruthie hadn't expected her to. Celeste knew her too well. She knew without being told that Ruthie could not compromise when it came to family. A job, yes. The hotel, maybe. But family? Children? Impossible.

"So what are you gonna do?"

She didn't know. It seemed foolish to continue down the road of a relationship that wasn't going anywhere. But could she give him up? Never see him again? Never curl against him in bed and twine her fingers into his dark, thick hair?

Never feel so emotionally attached and physically fulfilled by another person as long as she lived?

Not for the first time that day, tears rose to Ruthie's eyes and she angrily dashed them away. "I'm sorry, I can't believe how emotional I've been lately."

"You're due," Celeste said. "You've been through an awful lot, honey, losing your dad so young, and working so hard to get into culinary school in France. Your mom getting married. Then all this with the hotel. And now man trouble. I'd say you're *overdue* for a little emotion."

AFTER CELESTE LEFT, Ruthie got herself together for the day, even mustering up the energy to answer some e-mail and pay some bills. She couldn't believe how distracted she'd been lately, even to the point of nearly forgetting to make her car payment. When she'd glanced at the little calendar in her checkbook and noticed the date, she'd hurriedly written out as many checks as she could afford and stuck them in the downstairs mail drop.

After she was finished, she still had the nagging suspicion she'd overlooked something. There was something else she was supposed to take care of. A dentist appointment? A tune-up for her car? Lunch with a friend? It was going to drive her crazy until she remembered!

Though it was nearly unheard of for her, Ruthie actually went back to bed and took a quick nap early that afternoon. She knew it was depression over her relationship with Robert that was making her feel so sleepy, but she simply couldn't get through the night at the restaurant without resting first.

Later, as she was taking a shower and then drying her hair to get ready for work, she thought about what Celeste had said. She chuckled over the honeymoon story. "Poor Dain."

That tweaked a memory in her brain, got a spark shooting around, but Ruthie just couldn't grab the thought as it whizzed by. Shrugging, she began putting on her makeup, staring at the dark circles under her eyes, which she tried to conceal with some foundation.

Celeste had been right. She really did look like hell. Then she thought about something else Celeste had said. How Ruthie was entitled to a little emotion.

How she was *overdue*.

Ruthie stared at her reflection in the mirror and saw her own eyes widen in shock as she remembered just what it was she'd forgotten. "Oh, please, no," she said aloud as she ran for the calendar she kept in a drawer beside her bed.

She scanned it quickly, looking for the red pen-marks in the previous months. Two weeks. Two weeks late. Ruthie dropped the calendar to the floor and sat heavily on the bed.

"The bitch really *is* a condom killer!"

BY FRIDAY NIGHT when he got back to Philadelphia, Robert was feeling like an animal who'd been taunted by food dangled outside his cage. He'd thought of nothing but Ruthie in the twelve days since he'd seen her. Hearing her voice on the phone wasn't enough, especially since every time he called, she almost sounded surprised—like she really hadn't expected to hear from him again. That didn't do a lot to make Robert feel better. The sooner he got back to her, the sooner he could convince Ruthie he wasn't going anywhere.

And the sooner he'd have that smile on his face again.

Everyone had noticed his recent bad mood, from his cleaning lady to the doorman at his apartment building. They'd all commented on it. James Winchester had come right out and asked Robert what the heck was the matter with him, and Robert had been completely honest in his response.

To his surprise, considering how the man had been trying to set Robert up with Monica, James was very supportive. For all his success, James Winchester had never lost sight of the one most important factor in his life: his family. Learning that Robert had met a woman he was serious about, he'd apparently forgotten all about any idea of pushing him in Monica's direction, and urged Robert to work things out with Ruthie.

Though Robert hadn't asked for the older man's advice, he'd offered it anyway. "Grab personal happiness with both hands, my friend, because everything else in your life—career, financial success, everything—is just the topping on the sundae. Your home life is the ice cream. And while you can eat a whole big bowl of vanilla ice cream without any topping at all, there's just no way to choke down an entire jar of butterscotch sauce all by itself without gagging on it."

Robert had found himself smiling at the older man's analogy all week. So he was going to do something about it. He was going to ask Ruthie to move to New York and live with him. He even had visions of the two of them getting married eventually. He didn't imagine she'd been thinking that far ahead, after only a whirlwind, month-long relationship.

He felt certain she'd agree. Once she saw that her family was going to be taken care of when Winchester Hotels took over the Kerrigan, Ruthie would be free. Free to follow her own heart, find her own happiness in New York with Robert, and not focus every bit of her energy on her family.

When he got into town late Friday evening, he went straight to Ruthie's place. He knew she wouldn't be home from work until close to midnight, but she'd given him a key before he'd left so he could let himself in. Feeling stale and tired from a long week of work, followed by the plane ride, Robert decided to take a shower. While taking off his suit and tie, he also felt himself shrugging off his job. His business. All the deals and meetings and mergers. Everything else.

He felt himself unwinding, dropping his guard which had seen him through the shark-infested waters back in New York for the past two weeks. And he wondered if James had been right. Was it really so easy to have the best of both worlds? Was the secret to happiness the ability to drop everything from the outside world at the door when you came to the place you considered home?

He did consider her place home, which was funny, when he thought about it. Her little apartment was half the size of his in New York, but it had a more welcoming, lived-in feel, from the haphazard stacks of cooking magazines on the coffee table to the photos that lined every wall. In contrast, his place, which he'd paid a fortune to have decorated, seemed foreign. Just four walls and some furniture. Quiet. Empty. Lonely. What he'd thought he wanted but now found unbearable.

Ruthie had left a note on the table, telling him to help himself to the casserole in the fridge. When he opened it, he grinned. Casserole? Well, maybe. But this was no egg noodles, ham and cream of chicken soup like his mama had taught him to make for the boys when he was a kid.

Settling down to eat a late-night dinner, Robert marveled at what Ruthie could do with some tenderloin, red wine and pasta. From what he'd sampled of her cooking both at home and at the restaurant, he felt certain she would be able to get a job with one of the finer restaurants in New York. He wanted to help her, wanted to see her fulfill all her dreams.

After he ate, Robert watched the clock, waiting for

her to come home. Shortly after eleven, he heard the key in the lock.

"You came," she said when she entered the apartment and pushed the door closed behind her.

"Was there ever any doubt?"

She nodded, and Robert saw the sheen of tears in her eyes.

"Ruthie? What's wrong?"

"Nothing's wrong. I'm just glad you're here. I haven't been sleeping well without you."

He gave her a wolfish grin. "Hope you're not *too* tired."

Instead of giving him a seductive laugh, she cupped her hand against his face. "Take me to bed, Robert, please."

He needed no second invitation. Lifting her into his arms, he caught her mouth in a deep, wet kiss as he walked to her room. She curled her arms around his neck, holding him tightly as he lowered her to the bed.

Though he was dying for her, he sensed by her mood that Ruthie wanted no fast, frantic, heated coupling like some they'd enjoyed. In the two weeks they'd spent together, he'd seen Ruthie's sexual awakening. He'd seen her ravenous and insatiable, wanting hot, hard sex that left them both sweaty and panting. And he'd seen her sweet and tender, wrapping herself around him in the early morning to love him awake.

Tonight her mood was strange. Gentle. Languorous. Tender. But also a little frantic. She touched him everywhere, running her flat palms over his skin as if feeling him for the first time. Robert found himself caught up in her sweet sighs and fleeting touches and aroused beyond belief by her demanding kisses and possessive caresses.

He followed her lead, gentling his touch when her body silently asked him to with a quiver or a sigh. Speeding the pace when she demanded it with a twist or a thrust.

He loved her long into the night leaving no room for talk or laughter.

She seemed to want it that way.

RUTHIE KNEW when she awoke Saturday morning that she was going to have to find a way to say goodbye. She didn't want to. She so wished she didn't have to. But she had to end it.

She'd been right. A visit to her doctor Thursday afternoon had confirmed her fear. She was pregnant. Judging by what the doctor said, she'd probably conceived that first night they were together. Her immediate reaction hadn't been panic about being unmarried and pregnant by a man who didn't want children. No, her initial thoughts had involved fear for the baby, given the champagne and cold pills Ruthie had consumed the night she'd met Robert. This might not have been the way she'd planned to have a child, but she already wanted and loved this baby with a fierceness that astonished her.

Her Ob-Gyn had set her mind at ease. Telling her he'd seen many babies conceived after too much of a good time, he assured her the baby would be fine as long as she treated her body well in the coming months.

Making love with Robert was treating her body about as well as she could ever have dreamed. But it had to be the last time. Robert didn't want children. Ruthie did. They had no future together. It was that simple.

As much as she had fantasized in the past day or two about them working things out, she didn't want their child to be the reason he stayed with her. He'd never told her he loved her, never offered promises for any future together. But her pregnancy would put him in a corner. She wasn't willing to see the look she feared would be in his eyes—panic, dismay, or anger...then acceptance. Knowing him as she felt she did, she knew what he'd do. Be honorable. Noble. Self-sacrificing. She was worth more than that. So was their child.

So she couldn't tell him.

Not telling him was dishonest. Forcing him to make a choice he'd regret later was unfair. But when it came right down to it, having to live with a guilty conscience for deceiving him was better than saddling him with an instant family he'd never wanted in the first place.

She hadn't told anyone else about her pregnancy yet, either, still not sure how she was going to explain why she was having this baby alone. Celeste would be a great help. Her aunts and uncle would likely be distressed, and her mother mortified. But she couldn't think about that, about them. She had to think about the baby and their future together—a future which, unfortunately, didn't include his father. Funny, she already pictured the baby as a boy. A brown-eyed, dark-haired boy who would break her heart a little every day as he grew up to be the image of his father.

She really couldn't wait to meet him.

"YOU'RE UP EARLY," Robert said when she tried to slip out of bed Saturday morning. "Have lots of plans for us today?"

She was tempted to say yes. She wanted to grab this last day or two, hoping they'd remain in her memory for a long time. But that felt like stealing. Last night had been bad enough; she couldn't let an entire weekend go by without letting him know she was going to end their relationship.

"Actually, no," she said softly. "I was hoping we could have breakfast and talk this morning."

She didn't know exactly what she was going to say and prayed she could find the words to say goodbye. "I've been doing a lot of thinking since you left."

"Yeah, me too. I've missed you. I don't like us living hundreds of miles away from one another."

Ruthie was putting her robe on, but paused, one arm in one sleeve, at his words. "Really?"

"Really." He reached out his hand and pulled her closer, tugging her down to lie across his chest so he could kiss her. "I'm crazy about you," he said when she ended the kiss. "And I want you in my life permanently."

She held her breath, searching his eyes. Waiting.

"Come live with me in New York."

Ruthie pushed herself off his chest and moved to sit beside him, disappointment making her hands shake. "Live with you."

"Why not? Ruthie, you could do so much more than you're doing. There are restaurants that would kill to have someone as talented as you. And there are so many places to explore." He offered her a boyish smile. "I'd even sit through some Broadway musicals occasionally now that *Cats* has finally closed. There are amazing museums and galleries in New York. We could travel anywhere, the beaches or the ski slopes. Just be together."

She shook her head. He talked of travel and musicals when her immediate future was filled with cribs and diapers. She looked for other barriers, unwilling to voice her real concern. "What about the Kerrigan? My family needs me."

He shook his head. "You don't have to take care of them anymore. Your uncle, cousins and aunts will be fine. James has been very generous about letting them keep their positions. Except your uncle. There will have to be a new general manager, but Henry can retain a seat on the board."

Ruthie stared down at him, thoroughly confused. "What are you talking about? James who?"

"Winchester. I met with him several times over the past two weeks, telling him how important it is for your family to remain involved with the hotel after we take it over. And he agreed. He's not an ogre."

A slow realization finally pierced the hazy, pregnancy-filled recesses of Ruthie's mind. "Take it over?"

He obviously saw the horrified expression on her face. "Ruthie? What's the matter? I thought you'd be pleased."

She stood, walking across the room with her arms wrapped tightly around her waist. All these weeks she'd assumed it was done, the threat to the hotel ended. As if her pregnancy and her relationship with Robert weren't enough to worry about! And now... "You mean you're going ahead with it. You are going to force us to sell or risk losing the Kerrigan outright."

"Ruthie, you knew about this from the very beginning. Why are you looking so shocked?"

She stared at him from across the room, holding up one hand, palm-out, to stop him when he moved to get up. "Let me ask you one question. Did you intentionally mislead me? Or am I just so stupid I misunderstood what you meant when you said you wanted to do the *right thing* for my family."

He looked stunned. She had to give him that much. "Okay, I guess it was my stupidity," she said before he could reply.

"Ruthie, you thought..."

"Yeah," she said with a bitter laugh. "I thought you had finally gotten it. That you really did understand what it meant to be loyal to your loved ones, to have roots. I was obviously mistaken."

This time, her outstretched palm didn't stop him from getting up and walking across the floor to her. He was naked, sleepy and tousled and Ruthie had to firm up her resolve against him when he tried to pull her into his arms. "Don't."

"I didn't want your family hurt, Ruthie, but you have to understand. If it's not Winchester, it'll be someone else. You Sinclairs can't hold the hotel by yourselves. I thought I was helping by getting James to agree to my proposal."

"So I'm supposed to feel better that it's the man I *love* handing my family's heritage, practically my home, over to a corporate shark?" She regretted the words as soon as she spoke them, especially when she saw the quick flash of pleasure Robert was unable to disguise. "Forget I said that."

"Right. I'll just put it right out of my mind that the woman I'm crazy about loves me," he said with a pleased grin.

It was close. But it wasn't a declaration. She heard the difference, noted the distinction. He didn't appear to. "It doesn't matter."

"Hell yes, it matters! You and I definitely matter." He pressed a kiss to her lips, then said, "Please, Ruthie, let it go, let the hotel go. It's just a place. Trust me when I tell you the Sinclairs are going to be fine. We can be each other's family, Ruthie. Just you and me with no one else to answer to, responsible only for ourselves and free to do whatever we want."

He took a step back, then tipped her chin up, forcing her to look at him. "Come with me. Live with me. Let it happen."

The tender, passionate look in his eyes nearly broke her heart. But what he'd said reaffirmed what she already knew.

He didn't understand. Robert didn't recognize the importance of roots, history, family and loyalty. He wanted freedom. No encumbrances. She knew she probably should be flattered he was going so far as to ask her to share his life. That was a major step for him.

But it wasn't enough. How could he be a father to her baby? How could she rely on him to be part of a family with her and their child? If home was just a place to him, and he wanted freedom, no encumbrances, was it fair to try to tie him down?

"I'm sorry, Robert. The answer is no."

12

ROBERT LEFT an hour later, after trying unsuccessfully to change Ruthie's mind. For the first time in his life he found himself completely unable to say the right thing. Reason didn't work. Anger didn't work. Finally, accusing her of caring more about a place than she did about the life they could have together, he'd grabbed his things and slammed out.

He couldn't believe things had gone so wrong so quickly. He *really* couldn't believe Ruthie had chosen the pile of bricks that made up the Kerrigan Towers over her feelings for him.

That's what it felt like. A choice had been made. And she'd chosen the place, not the man.

He drove to the airport, figuring he might as well fly back to New York. He couldn't stay around Philadelphia, hoping she'd change her mind. Robert wondered why he even wanted her to when he was so damned angry with her anyway.

Going back to New York didn't seem the answer either. When he got to the ticket counter, for some reason he found himself asking the agent to book him a flight to Charlotte, instead.

He didn't worry about what kind of reception he'd get from his parents. They were always pestering him to come visit, though he seldom did except during the holidays. Now, however, he sensed there was nowhere else he could go.

ALL HER LIFE, Ruthie Sinclair had been a cryer. She cried at movies, she cried at Kodak commercials, she cried at sappy love songs. She cried at weddings and while reading her favorite romance novels.

But that weekend, she didn't cry. At least not *much*.

She was too unhappy. The pain went too deep. Superficial tears couldn't express her sorrow at pushing Robert away.

That didn't mean she wasn't still furious with him. "The man is dense," she muttered to herself Sunday morning while she wandered aimlessly around her apartment, wondering why he'd given up and left, though she'd demanded he do just that.

She couldn't blame him for being who he was. His job had come first. He'd pushed ahead with business, and thrust aside personal relationships. He hadn't understood her at all. Those were the basic facts, ones she was going to have to learn to live with. The lesson had been tough—blistering. And it had left her changed forever.

Though her stomach was still flat—well, as flat as her stomach ever was, and that was never completely bikini flat—she found herself stroking her belly, murmuring to her baby. "I'm sorry. I should have tried for you, shouldn't I?"

She still hadn't figured out exactly what she was going to say to Uncle Henry about the Kerrigan. She didn't know how he would take the news that she'd been wrong and Robert's company was going to force them to sell after all. They'd wasted precious weeks when they could have been looking for another option, all because she hadn't pressed Robert for details, hadn't wanted to look any deeper than the obvious solution that he cared for her too much to hurt her family.

If she had, maybe they would have been able to find someone else to refinance their mortgage. But if she had, maybe she and Robert wouldn't have had those two magical weeks together.

"Was it worth it?" she asked her reflection as she prepared to go to meet with Henry at the hotel Sunday afternoon.

She really didn't know.

HER UNCLE took the news better than she would ever have expected. All of them did, from Henry to Elise, even the aunts. Ruthie had to wonder just how much they knew about her relationship with Robert Kendall, especially as Uncle Henry looked at her with gentleness and love when she told him she'd been wrong, that they were still backed in a corner.

She suspected he knew by her pale, pinched face, and by the words she didn't say, that her heart ached over more than the potential loss of the Kerrigan.

Celeste certainly knew. On Tuesday afternoon, she met Ruthie in the lobby, took her by the arm and practically dragged her to her office. "What happened? I took a sick day yesterday and came back to hear the vultures are circling again."

Ruthie sat heavily on a chair in the office. "I misunderstood. He never intended to back away from the deal. He never even understood why I would be so heartbroken by it."

Celeste grabbed a tissue, obviously expecting Ruthie to dissolve into tears, but Ruthie couldn't manage even a sniffle.

"That snake. Using you, misleading you."

"He didn't mean to."

Celeste snorted.

"No, I heard what I wanted to hear. And I know he feels terrible about it."

Celeste still looked skeptical. "Sure he does."

"He asked me to move to New York and live with him."

"What?" her cousin shrieked as she jumped up from behind her desk and hurried to close the door of her office. "Spill!"

"He said after the hotel changes hands my family would be well taken care of and I would be free to come live with him."

"And you said...?"

"I said no."

Celeste nodded thoughtfully. "Yes, of course, you would."

"What's that supposed to mean?"

"No offense, Ruthie. But it's just typical of you to go the safe way, stay near home, focus on the family."

Ruthie heard no condemnation in her cousin's voice, though she did see by Celeste's slight frown that her cousin was disappointed in her. "You think I should have gone?"

Celeste shrugged. "I don't know. I think you should have seriously thought about it. And I definitely don't think you should have let the hotel be the reason you said no."

"It wasn't just the hotel." Ruthie really hadn't intended to tell her cousin about the pregnancy, but she felt like she was going to explode if she didn't tell someone. "I can't just quit my job and go off to live in a strange city because I now have a baby to think about."

Celeste's face paled and her mouth fell open. "Baby?"

After Ruthie told her everything, Celeste cried a bit. Then she took Ruthie in her arms and hugged her, murmuring words that did nothing to help. When she realized that Ruthie was not hysterical, not about to burst into tears, she sat on the edge of her desk and looked down at her. "How did he react?"

"I didn't tell him."

Celeste frowned. "Why not?"

"I can't trap him. I know his stand on kids and family."

"His *stand*?" Celeste shook her head in confusion. "Too bad about his *stand*, Ruthie. He lost the right to have a *stand* the night that baby was conceived...by *both* of you."

"I can raise this baby by myself, Celeste."

"You of all people should know what it's like not to have a father. At least you were lucky enough to have yours for the first seventeen years of your life. And you're telling me you're denying your baby the chance to have one at all?"

She winced. That was hitting below the belt. Celeste knew full well how devastating her father's death had been to Ruthie. "I can't force Robert to have a family he doesn't want," she finally muttered.

"So don't. You don't have to force him to do a single thing. What you do have to do is give your baby a chance to have a father." Celeste knelt by Ruthie's chair. "Give the man you tell me you love the chance to show what he's made of. Get your head around the idea that nothing—not the Kerrigan, not the Sinclairs, not history or money or a job—is as important as the kind of future you can give my godchild."

SHE BOOKED A FLIGHT to New York the next morning. There were some things that simply couldn't be said over the phone. Telling Robert he was going to be a father definitely qualified.

Ruthie had to see for herself, in the moment the words came out of her mouth, how he truly felt about it. She would be able to tell by his eyes, by the look on his face. That would determine how she would handle everything that followed.

Ruthie packed a few things in an overnight bag and called to book a hotel room in New York. She knew Celeste was right and she had to respect Robert enough to let him decide for himself how to handle her pregnancy. That didn't mean she was going to crash in on him, unannounced, and expect him to be happy about it.

Stopping by the hotel on her way to the airport, she went to the restaurant to make sure things would be covered for a few days. Assured by her staff that they had everything under control, she walked back to the lobby, trying to build up her courage to go through with the trip.

She was looking at her feet, a strange thought zipping across her mind that in a few months she wouldn't be able to see them anymore, when she ran into someone.

"Robert?" She couldn't believe it was him. After all the hormone-inspired emotions, she just couldn't quite believe her eyes when she saw him standing directly in front of her, steadying her as she wobbled from their collision.

"You really do need to watch where you're going, sugar."

She ignored him. "You came back. More meetings?"

"Only one that matters," he said as he took her arm and led her none-too-gently toward the exit.

"Where are you taking me?"

"You're not going to work. They can serve frozen dinners tonight for all I care. Ruthie, you and I are going to talk."

Ruthie followed helplessly while he walked her around the side of the building to the pool. Only a few hotel guests basked in the late afternoon sun, and watched with barely concealed interest as Robert led Ruthie to a vacant table and pushed her into a chair. "Now, just listen. Okay?"

She nodded.

"You were right."

"I was?"

"Yeah, Ruthie, you were. I didn't understand. I felt like you were choosing the Kerrigan over a future with me, and I didn't see—didn't *let* myself see—why it mattered so much."

Ruthie chewed the corner of her lip, afraid to get her hopes up. But her heart pounded wildly. "Go on."

"I was being unreasonable. It wasn't until I went back home and spent some time with my family that I recognized it."

"You went to North Carolina?"

He nodded, a slow smile crossing his face. "My parents almost fell off the porch swing when I pulled up in a taxi."

Ruthie had a vision of his family, the whole loud bunch of them, living in a pretty little southern house that was bursting at the seams with children and grandchildren. "I'm sure they were happy you came."

"My mother knew something was wrong within five

minutes. Her solution involved copious amounts of food."

"Woman after my own heart," Ruthie murmured.

"Anyway, the point is, spending a few days with my family reminded me of my roots. How hard my parents worked on their business, how much they sacrificed. If some out-of-state money man came in and tried to force them to sell out, I guess I'd be feeling just as devastated as you've been."

This time, she allowed her hopes to build. He sounded like he really meant it. It wasn't a vague hope he'd find a way to save the Kerrigan for the Sinclairs that made her feel like such a weight had been lifted from her shoulders. It was simply the fact that he understood—he was acknowledging her feelings and empathizing with them. "You mean that?"

He nodded his head and gave her a sad smile. "God, I'm sorry, Ruthie. I'm so sorry for not taking a single minute to put myself in your shoes. I decided I knew how you should react to what I had planned for our future and didn't stop to think that you might feel differently."

Ruthie's hand dropped from the table down to her lap and she pressed her palm to her stomach. Robert was guilty of no more than she'd been and he'd had the courage to say so right to her face. She could do nothing less, no matter what it cost her. "I'm glad you came back. I needed to see you. I was actually planning to fly up to New York."

He looked pleased by her admission. "There was no question that I was coming back, Ruthie."

"Because of the hotel?"

He rolled his eyes. "No, not because of the hotel. Because of you. If you thought one argument was going to make me walk away from you forever, you don't know me very well."

"I wasn't going to *let* you walk away without having this conversation. We need to lay all the cards on the table now. Be completely honest with each other." She took another deep breath and crossed her fingers.

"In that case, there's something else you don't know about me, about my family," he said, "and I think you ought to."

She grinned, remembering their very first conversation. "I know you're not married, not gay and not a sissy mama's boy."

"No," he said with a laugh. "But when I told you my parents were in the auto repair business, I don't know if I ever made it clear to you that they're pretty darn successful at it."

"Really? I always pictured them as struggling to get by."

"They did, when I was growing up. They put every penny and all their energy into their shops."

"Shops?"

Robert nodded. "They now own forty-seven of them throughout the Carolinas and Georgia."

Ruthie's mouth fell open. Robert tipped it closed with his index finger. "Not exactly struggling," she managed to say.

"Oh, no. And they gave part ownership in the company to me and all my brothers the day they opened the thirtieth location."

"You're rich?"

"I'm comfortable. My parents are rich. They're also very bored."

Confused, Ruthie tilted her head and raised an eyebrow.

He explained. "They liked the challenge, liked building something from the ground up. Now it's too easy and they're looking for a new project to take on."

She still wasn't getting him. "Okay. So, are they taking up mountain climbing? What?"

He leaned closer and took her hand in his. "They've been asking a lot of questions about the hotel industry."

She began to understand. "The Kerrigan..."

"Don't get upset. I haven't been making any under-the-table deals. I just mentioned this place, how wonderful it is. They started talking about how they were looking to diversify. Since I have the hotel-motel industry expertise, they were hoping I'd help them."

"They want to invest in this hotel?"

"Maybe. They want to form a new division, and they want me to head it up. They've mentioned it in passing for the past couple of years, but I never realized how serious they were about it. Or how much I wanted to do it."

"You really do?"

He nodded and smiled, looking almost surprised himself. "Yeah, I do. It'll be a challenging opportunity for me. And one of our first projects could be a *family* effort to restore the Kerrigan Towers and make it a showplace of Philadelphia."

"Family," she whispered.

"Your family. My family. Our family."

"Ours?"

"I know it's too soon, Ruthie. I know it is, and I didn't want to scare you off, which is why I asked you to move in with me. What I really picture is us getting married."

The tears that hadn't come for several days started

with a tiny trickle and Ruthie blinked rapidly to try to prevent a torrential onslaught. "You're asking me to marry you?"

He nodded. "Yes, I am. I love you. I've loved you from the night we met. I've never found such pleasure with another human being in my entire life, Ruthie. You've ruined me for anyone else, including myself. I can't be alone anymore."

He meant it. She saw it in his eyes, in the tender curve of his lips, in the rueful smile.

Robert brushed a strand of hair, caught by the breeze, off her brow and tucked it behind her ear. "I want to build a future with you. We can still have the world, Ruthie, side by side. But we can also have family and roots and all the things you've been trying to tell me I needed, too. We really *can* have it all. I've discovered that I *want* it all."

Ruthie held her breath. There was one thing he hadn't mentioned. One final hurdle. "Children?"

He grinned. "You know, my brothers' girls are so darn cute. There are four of them and, I tell you, in the past three days I have learned more about how to dress a Barbie doll than any grown, unmarried man should ever know."

She started to laugh even as the tears came faster. "So?"

"So, all I could think while I was trying to figure out how to get the stretchy spandex pants on this rubber-legged doll was that I would love someday to do the same thing with a little red-haired, green-eyed girl of my own."

That released the torrent. The tears slid down her cheeks in rivulets as Ruthie threw her arms around his neck. "I love you so much," she said as she pressed kisses on his cheek.

"I love you, too."

Then he was kissing her, pulling her off the chair until she sat on his lap, and Ruthie held him tight, unwilling to loosen her hold for fear this was all a dream. A lovely, intoxicating dream. If so, she hoped she never woke up.

Finally, when their lips broke apart, Ruthie tucked her head on his shoulder, gently kissing his earlobe. Taking his hand in hers, she moved it from her hip to the front of her body, feeling him cup her stomach. She held his hand tight.

"One question, Robert. Uh, exactly what do you consider 'someday'?"

_____ Epilogue _____

Two Months Later

"DON'T TRY to carry me over the threshold, Robert, I have already gained five pounds with this pregnancy. At the rate I'm going, I'll be a whale by Christmas!"

"Stop being so bossy, wife," Robert replied, looking with love into Ruthie's laughing green eyes. "This is once in a lifetime and I'm doing it right."

She giggled but didn't protest as he nudged the door to their suite open and carried her into it, tugging her long white satin train in after them. He kicked the door shut, then carried her over to the bed. "Sure you don't mind that we didn't get the same room where it all began?" he asked as he gently laid her on top of the thick, quilted bedspread.

"Not at all," she replied. "I was not about to wait another three months until the renovations on the fourth floor rooms were complete. This baby's going to do enough finger-counting when he's old enough to ask when our anniversary is in comparison to his birthday!"

"*She* won't care about that, it'll just reiterate how much in love her parents were...even before the wedding."

"I'd love to give you a daughter, sweetheart, but my heart tells me I'm carrying a perfect baby boy. A darling little brown-haired, brown-eyed baby boy."

Robert shook his head. "Uh-uh. Red-haired, green-eyed girl, darlin'." Robert saw the bottle of sparkling cider resting in an ice bucket on the desk, along with a note. "From my parents," he said. "They're crazy about you, you know."

Ruthie nodded, a self-satisfied smile on her face. "All it took was my chicken-fried steak to win over your dad. Your mom was a tougher nut."

Robert snorted. "Nah, all it took for her was finding out you had finally cured me of my whole anti-baby thing."

Ruthie gasped. "Robert! No one was supposed to know about the baby until after the wedding. What must she think?"

Crossing the room, Robert sat down on the bed beside her and pressed a gentle kiss to her temple. "Sweetheart, she and dad stayed here for two weeks before they became part owners of the Kerrigan, remember? She obviously knew we were *involved*. Did you really think the whole linen closet episode was going to remain a staff secret?"

He loved the rush of pink flooding into Ruthie's cheeks.

"Don't worry, she's just so excited about having a new grandbaby, she's certainly not going to criticize the timing."

"Well, now that I've met all your brothers and their families, I can understand why. You Kendalls do create beautiful children. Joey's and Lenny's girls look enough alike to be sisters, not cousins."

"That's understandable, since Joey and Lenny are twins."

Ruthie's eyes widened. "Twins? Why didn't I know that? Twins run in your family?"

He nodded, wondering why she was so interested. "Sorry, I never mentioned it. No big deal, they're not identical and a lot of people don't even notice."

"Fraternal twins," Ruthie said softly, twisting the gold band he'd placed on her finger hours before. "Funny. You do know my father was Uncle Henry's twin...older by ten minutes."

Robert nodded, tenderly kissing her hand. "I'm sure that made today doubly special since Henry gave you away."

She nodded, still deep in thought. "And Aunts Lila and Flossie."

"Those two are *twins*? I never would have guessed that!"

She sucked in her bottom lip and gave him a look of wide-eyed innocence.

"Ruthie? What's wrong?"

"It was just a little echo, I'm quite sure."

"Echo?"

"The doctor heard something when he was trying to pick up the baby's heartbeat at my visit this week. An echo. I'll bet that's all it was. Or else, it was faulty equipment. Yes, that would explain why it sounded like there were two heartbeats."

She nodded, then lay back on the bed, curling up against him. Sliding his arms around her shoulders, he pulled her close to his chest. As always, Robert was slightly awed by the power of his feelings for her. Then what she'd said sunk in.

"*Two?*"

She nodded sleepily against his chest.

Twins? Robert just stared wide-eyed at the ceiling for a minute, trying to absorb the concept. When a grin forced his lips wide, and a chuckle erupted from his mouth, he realized he could handle it. Two little Ruthies. Two beautiful red-haired angels with laughing green eyes who would have their daddy wrapped around their fingers.

He could handle that. He could definitely handle that.

THE TWINS—a red-haired, green-eyed boy and a brown-haired, brown-eyed girl—were born five months later. As he left the hospital with his new family, Robert smiled at the woman he adored and said, "We'll guess the colors right the next time, sugar."

It's hot...and it's out of control.

BLAZE

*This winter is going to be hot, hot, hot!
Don't miss these bold, provocative,
ultra-sexy books!*

SEDUCED by Janelle Denison
December 2000

Lawyer Ryan Matthews wanted sexy Jessica Newman the
moment he saw her. And she seemed to want him, too, but
something was holding her back. So Ryan decides it's time
to launch a sensual assault. He *is* going to have Jessica in
his bed—and he isn't above tempting her with her own
forbidden fantasies to do it....

SIMPLY SENSUAL by Carly Phillips
January 2001

When P.I. Ben Callahan agrees to take the job of watching
over spoiled heiress Grace Montgomery, he figures it's easy
money. That is, until he discovers gorgeous Grace has a
reckless streak a mile wide and is a serious threat to his
libido—and his heart. Ben isn't worried about keeping
Grace safe. But can he protect her from his loving lies?

Don't miss this daring duo!

HARLEQUIN®
Temptation.

Visit us at www.eHarlequin.com   HTBLAZEW

Tyler Brides

It happened one weekend...

Quinn and Molly Spencer are delighted to accept three
bookings for their newly opened B&B, Breakfast Inn Bed,
located in America's favorite hometown, Tyler, Wisconsin.

But Gina Santori is anything but thrilled to discover her
best friend has tricked her into sharing a room with
the man who broke her heart eight years ago....

And Delia Mayhew can hardly believe that she's
gotten herself locked in the Breakfast Inn Bed
basement with the sexiest man in America.

Then there's Rebecca Salter. She's turned up at the
Inn in her wedding gown. Minus her groom.

*Come home to Tyler for three delightful novellas
by three of your favorite authors: Kristine Rolofson,
Heather MacAllister and Jacqueline Diamond.*

HARLEQUIN®
Makes any time special ™

Visit us at www.eHarlequin.com

PHTB

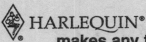

Pamela Burford presents

The Wedding Ring

*Four high school friends and a pact—
every girl gets her ideal mate by thirty or be
prepared for matchmaking! The rules are
simple. Give your "chosen" man three
months...and see what happens!*

Love's Funny That Way
Temptation #812—on sale December 2000
It's no joke when Raven Muldoon falls in love with comedy
club owner Hunter—*brother* of her "intended."

I Do, But Here's the Catch
Temptation #816—on sale January 2001
Charli Ross is more than willing to give up her status as
last of a dying breed—the thirty-year-old virgin—to Grant.
But all *he* wants is marriage.

One Eager Bride To Go
Temptation #820—on sale February 2001
Sunny Bleecker is still waiting tables at Wafflemania when
Kirk comes home from California and wants to marry her.
It's as if all her dreams have finally come true—except...

Fiancé for Hire
Temptation #824—on sale March 2001
No way is Amanda Coppersmith going to let
The Wedding Ring rope her into marriage. But no matter
how clever she is, Nick is one step ahead of her...

*"Pamela Burford creates the
memorable characters readers love!"
—The Literary Times*